Bigfoot
Trackless

by Ethan Blackwood

Copyright @2025
Ethan Blakwood

Chapter 1 – Inaugural Night

The air in the Anchorage Grand Terminal thrummed with a manicured excitement, a symphony of hushed awe and the bright, percussive clicks of camera shutters. It was an atmosphere thick with the scent of expensive perfume, chilled champagne, and the faint, metallic tang of new beginnings. Outside, the Alaskan twilight, a bruised purple deepening to indigo, was held at bay by the brilliant halogen glow that bathed the sleek, silver flanks of The Borealis Express. This was not merely a train; it was a statement, a rolling testament to opulence, a steel ambassador sent to conquer the last vestiges of true wilderness with five-star amenities and curated Instagram moments.

Tonight was its inaugural journey, a ribbon-cutting spectacle years and billions in the making. The brainchild of eccentric tech billionaire Alistair Prichard, a man whose fortune was built on predicting what people wanted before they knew it themselves, The Borealis Express promised an unprecedented passage through Alaska's most remote and myth-steeped landscapes. Untouched, the brochures had screamed in elegant serif font, Unforgettable.

Quinn Mallory felt decidedly out of place amidst the glittering throng. Her invitation, a glossy, heavyweight cardstock that probably cost more than her monthly grocery bill, had arrived like a missive from an alternate reality. "Congratulations, Winner of the 'Wild Heart of

Alaska' Essay Contest!" it had declared. Her essay, a heartfelt, slightly academic piece on the delicate balance of predator-prey relationships in the Alaskan interior, had apparently struck a chord. Or, more likely, her name had been pulled from a very small, very specific hat. She clutched a complimentary flute of champagne, the bubbles tickling her nose, and tried to look like she belonged, a task made more difficult by the fact her dress was off-the-rack and her shoes were chosen for comfort over couture.

Around her, the other passengers were a dazzling, slightly terrifying menagerie. There was Prichard himself, holding court near the primary boarding ramp, a wiry man with eyes that seemed to absorb light and a smile that never quite reached them. He was flanked by a rotating cast of what Quinn assumed were other billionaires, men and women with tans that spoke of leisure in sunnier climes and voices that carried the easy authority of those unaccustomed to being told 'no'.

Then there were the influencers, a flock of brightly plumed birds, their movements quick and performative. Quinn recognized a few from the periphery of her social media feeds. Lila Vance, a lifestyle vlogger whose entire existence seemed to be a meticulously curated pastel dream, was currently orchestrating a Boomerang of herself clinking champagne flutes with two other women whose faces were immobile masks of practiced joy. Their laughter, high and brittle, punctuated the general murmur. They were all impossibly slender, their hair artfully tousled, their outfits a coordinated assault of designer labels. Nature, Quinn suspected, was merely a backdrop for their next sponsored post.

"Isn't it just breathtaking?" A voice, smooth as silk, startled Quinn. She turned to see a woman with a cascade of silver hair and a kind, if slightly weary, smile. This was Eleanor Ainsworth, the train's General Manager, a figure of calm efficiency amidst the barely contained chaos. "Alistair has truly outdone himself this time."

"It's... a lot," Quinn admitted, then winced internally. Eloquence had apparently deserted her.

Eleanor's smile widened. "That it is. But spectacular, don't you think? We're hoping to redefine luxury travel. And to open up this incredible part of the world, responsibly, of course."

Quinn nodded, taking another sip of champagne. The word 'responsibly' hung in the air, feeling a little thin against the sheer, unapologetic extravagance of the train itself. Each carriage was a bespoke marvel, from the panoramic viewing cars with their domed ceilings of reinforced glass to the dining car that boasted a Michelin-starred chef, Bruno, a burly, temperamental Italian who had been lured away from his Tuscan villa by an obscene sum and the promise of caribou tartare.

A subtle shift in the crowd's energy indicated a new arrival. A hush fell, quickly replaced by a fresh flurry of camera flashes. An older man, his face a roadmap of wrinkles, his bearing proud and solemn, was being escorted towards Alistair Prichard by a nervous-looking PR aide. He wore traditional Athabascan attire, intricately beaded and fringed, a stark contrast to Prichard's tailored European suit.

"Ladies and gentlemen," Prichard's voice, amplified by a discreet microphone, cut through the chatter. "It is my distinct honor to welcome Mr. Elias Prichard, an elder of the K'eyghot'an people, whose ancestral lands we will soon be privileged to witness." He made a grand, sweeping gesture towards the train. "Mr. Prichard, we are deeply grateful for your presence and your blessing on this historic voyage."

Elias Prichard (no relation, the PR aide had hastily clarified to a journalist earlier) stepped forward. He did not smile. His gaze, dark and penetrating, swept over the assembled crowd, lingering for a moment on the gleaming train before returning to Alistair. When he spoke, his voice was low, resonant, carrying an unexpected weight that silenced even the most determined networkers.

"This land," he began, his English careful, accented, "is not a picture. It is not a playground for the wealthy." His eyes seemed to find Quinn in the crowd, a brief, assessing glance. "It has a memory, long and deep. It remembers those who walk softly upon it, and those who do not." He paused, and the silence stretched, taut and uncomfortable. "The Borealis Express," he said, the name sounding foreign on his tongue. "It cuts a new path. Paths that are not asked for are seldom welcome for long."

He then produced a small, carved wooden amulet, shaped like a raven. He did not offer it to Prichard, but instead held it out towards the train itself, his lips moving in a silent incantation. The air around him seemed to grow colder for a moment. Then, he turned, not to Prichard, but to the PR aide. "I will not board," he stated, his voice firm.

"My journey ends here. May you find what you seek, though I fear what it might be." With that, he turned and, with a dignity that brooked no argument, walked away from the lights, away from the train, melting back into the Alaskan shadows from whence he came.

Alistair Prichard, after a microsecond of visible surprise, recovered with a practiced laugh. "A man of strong convictions! We respect that. We respect the traditions." He clapped his hands together. "Well then! To the Borealis Express! Let the adventure begin!"

The crowd, after a moment of awkward hesitation, rallied with a cheer, the elder's unsettling words already fading, dismissed as quaint local color. Champagne flowed anew. The influencers, after a brief, confused pause where they clearly debated if the elder's departure was 'content', decided against it and resumed their posing. Lila Vance was now trying to get a shot of herself looking thoughtfully out at the distant mountains, her expression one of profound, if manufactured, contemplation.

Quinn, however, felt a chill that had nothing to do with the Alaskan air. *The land remembers.*

Boarding was an exercise in organized opulence. Velvet ropes, obsequious staff in crisp, dark green uniforms emblazoned with a stylized gold 'BE', and the low hum of the train's powerful engines, eager to be unleashed. Quinn found her cabin in the 'Aurora Sleeper' car. It was compact but exquisitely appointed: polished dark wood, plush teal upholstery, a surprisingly comfortable bed that folded down from the wall, and a picture window that promised breathtaking views. A small, leather-bound journal and a silver pen lay on the small writing desk, a thoughtful touch.

She stowed her single duffel bag – a stark contrast to the mountains of designer luggage being manhandled by porters in the corridor – and took a moment to simply breathe. The train gave a gentle sigh, a release of air brakes, and then, with a barely perceptible tremor, began to move.

Smooth. Unbelievably smooth. It was less like a train and more like gliding. Quinn pressed her face to the cool glass of the window. Anchorage, with its grid of lights, began to recede, giving way to the darkening expanse of the wilderness. Trees, skeletal against the fading light, massed into dense forests. Mountains, their peaks already dusted with early snow, loomed like sleeping giants.

Later, in the 'Midnight Sun' observation car, the atmosphere was one of forced conviviality. The domed glass roof offered a staggering vista of the night sky. The aurora borealis had decided to put on a show, shimmering curtains of green and violet light dancing across the velvet blackness. It was a spectacle of such profound, otherworldly beauty that it almost, almost, silenced the chatter.

Almost.

"Hashtag Northern Lights! Hashtag Blessed!" chirped a young man with aggressively blond hair, his phone held aloft, live-streaming to his legion of followers. "Guys, you would not *believe* this. It's, like, literally insane. Make sure you smash that like button!"

Lila Vance, having changed into a silver sequined dress that seemed to compete with the aurora itself, was holding court with a rapt audience of two other influencers and a paunchy man Quinn vaguely recognized as a software mogul. "…and so I told my agent, if the brand synergy isn't authentic, then what's the point, you know? My followers, they trust my authenticity." She gestured vaguely towards the celestial display. "This, for example. Totally authentic. Pure nature. My next reel is going to be epic."

Quinn found a quiet corner, nursing a glass of water. She watched them, these people who lived their lives through screens, who seemed to experience the world only as a series of potential photo opportunities. She wondered if they even saw the aurora, or if they just saw the likes it would generate.

The train sped on, a silver bullet piercing the heart of the wilderness. The forests grew denser, the mountains more imposing. There were no roads out here, no settlements, just mile upon mile of untamed land. The silence outside the train, Quinn imagined, must be immense, profound. Inside, the bubble of human noise and artificial light felt increasingly incongruous, an affront to the ancient stillness.

She thought of the elder, Elias Prichard. *Paths that are not asked for are seldom welcome for long.*

Hours passed. The champagne continued to flow. Some of the older billionaires had retired to their cabins. The influencers, however, seemed to possess inexhaustible energy, fueled by caffeine and the relentless pursuit of content. Quinn watched Lila attempt to teach the software mogul a TikTok dance, a scene of such awkwardness it was almost painful.

The train's chef, Bruno, made a brief, theatrical appearance, his white toque immaculate, his expression one of weary disdain as he surveyed the revelers. He exchanged a few curt words with Eleanor Ainsworth, then retreated to his culinary domain, presumably to prepare for the midnight oyster bar.

Quinn felt a growing unease, a subtle thrum beneath the surface of the forced gaiety. It was more than just the elder's words. It was the sheer arrogance of it all, this luxurious intrusion into a world that had existed for millennia without human interference on this scale. The train, for all its technological marvel, felt fragile against the backdrop of such immense, indifferent wilderness.

She noticed the subtle sway of the carriage increasing slightly. The rhythmic clack-clack of the wheels on the rails, usually a soothing sound, seemed to have a harder, more urgent edge. Or was she imagining it? She glanced out the window. The trees were a black, impenetrable wall, rushing past in a blur. The aurora had faded, leaving the sky a star-dusted canvas of deepest indigo.

She decided to head back to her cabin. The party atmosphere was beginning to feel oppressive. As she excused herself, navigating a gauntlet of air kisses and oblivious selfie-takers, she caught the eye of Hammond, the train's chief engineer. He was a stocky man in his late fifties, his face weathered, his expression usually one of quiet competence. Tonight, though, there was a faint line of worry etched between his brows. He was standing near one of the service doors, speaking in low tones to a member of his crew, occasionally glancing out the window with a frown. Quinn offered a small smile, which he returned with a distracted nod.

Back in the quiet sanctuary of her cabin, Quinn changed into her pajamas and pulled down the bed. The journal lay on the desk. She picked it up, then set it down again. What could she possibly write? *Day one: surrounded by people who communicate primarily through hashtags. Wilderness is pretty. Felt vaguely doomed.*

She opted for a book she'd brought, a well-worn collection of Robert Service poems. The rhythmic cadence of "The Cremation of Sam McGee" was a familiar comfort. She read for a while, the gentle rocking of the train usually a soporific. But tonight, sleep felt distant. The elder's words echoed in her mind. *The land remembers.*

She must have dozed off, book slipping from her fingers, because the next thing she knew, she was jolted awake by a sound, a sensation, that ripped through the fabric of the night.

BANG.

It wasn't just a sound; it was a physical blow, a monstrous, metallic shriek that seemed to come from the very soul of the train. The carriage bucked violently, throwing Quinn sideways. Her head cracked against the wooden paneling of the wall with a sickening thud. For a disoriented moment, stars exploded behind her eyelids, not the celestial kind, but sharp, painful bursts of light.

The train, which moments before had been a smooth, gliding dream, was now a bucking bronco. Emergency lights flickered on, casting the narrow corridor outside her partially open door in a ghastly, strobing red. Screams, sharp and terrified, pierced the sudden, deafening silence that followed the initial impact. The rhythmic clatter of the wheels was gone, replaced by a horrifying, grinding screech of metal on metal, then a series of violent, bone-jarring jolts.

Quinn scrambled up, her heart hammering against her ribs, a wave of nausea washing over her. The floor was tilted at a crazy angle. Her book had slid across the room. The champagne flute, miraculously intact on her small nightstand, teetered and then crashed to the floor, shattering with a delicate, incongruous chime.

Then, as suddenly as it began, the violent motion ceased. The train shuddered to a complete, dead stop.

Silence. A thick, ringing silence, broken only by the distant, panicked shouts of passengers and the closer, more immediate sound of someone in the next cabin sobbing hysterically. The emergency lights pulsed, red, red, red, painting the world in shades of alarm.

Quinn, her hands shaking, pulled herself to her feet, using the wall for support. The train was definitely tilted. Outside her window, there was only blackness, the dense, impenetrable black of the Alaskan night, now made more terrifying by the unnatural stillness.

What had happened? Had they hit something? Derailed?

Her training, the ingrained instincts of someone who had spent time in unpredictable environments, began to kick in, cutting through the initial shock. *Assess. Don't panic.*

Footsteps pounded in the corridor. Voices, urgent and strained.

"What was that?"

"Are we okay?"

"Somebody do something!"

Then, a new sound. A low, powerful hum, a vibration that started deep within the train and grew steadily. The lights flickered again, then steadied, the main power returning, banishing the demonic red glow. The train gave a sudden, violent lurch, accompanied by a groan of stressed metal that sounded almost human.

And then, with an agonizing slowness, The Borealis Express began to move. Not smoothly, not with its earlier confident glide, but with a hesitant, grinding effort, like a wounded animal dragging itself forward. The rhythmic clack-clack of the wheels returned, but it was uneven, labored, punctuated by disconcerting groans and creaks from the carriage structure.

Quinn gripped the edge of her small desk, her knuckles white. The train was moving, but something was terribly wrong. The impact, the sudden stop, the way it now struggled onward — it all pointed to something far more serious than a minor mechanical fault.

She looked out her window again. The impenetrable blackness slid past, but it felt different now, charged with a new menace. The wilderness, which had been a majestic backdrop, now seemed to press in on them, vast and indifferent to their plight.

The party, Quinn knew with a certainty that chilled her to the bone, was most definitely over. The inaugural night of The Borealis Express had taken a dark, terrifying turn, and out there, in the trackless, remembering land, something had made its presence known.

Chapter 2 – The Line Breaks

The Borealis Express, mortally wounded, crawled onward through the oppressive Alaskan dark. Each rotation of its damaged wheels was a torturous groan, a metallic lament that echoed through the tilted carriages. Inside, the initial shockwave of the impact had given way to a trembling, adrenaline-fueled anxiety. Quinn, still pressed against the cool wood paneling of her cabin, listened to the cacophony: the stuttering rhythm of the train, the distant, muffled shouts of crew trying to impose order, and the closer, more intimate sounds of fear – a woman weeping uncontrollably in the adjacent cabin, a man cursing in low, furious tones.

Her head throbbed where it had struck the wall, a dull ache that served as a constant reminder of the violence. The main lights, though restored, flickered intermittently, casting long, dancing shadows that made the already skewed perspectives of the listing carriage even more disorienting. The train was not just tilted; it felt fundamentally unstable, as if it might tear itself apart with every labored revolution.

Quinn forced herself to move. She checked her small duffel bag, ensuring her sturdy hiking boots and outdoor gear were still secure. Practicality over panic. That was the mantra. She had no illusions about her situation. Whatever had hit them, whatever was causing this agonizing, limping journey, was serious.

Cautiously, she opened her cabin door. The corridor was a scene of subdued chaos. A few passengers, pale and wide-eyed, clung to the handrails, their party attire looking absurdly out of place against the backdrop of fear. A crew member, a young man whose face was ashen, hurried past, muttering into a radio that seemed to crackle with more static than sense.

"Please return to your cabins," he said, his voice strained. "We are assessing the situation. Please remain calm."

Calm. It seemed an impossible request.

Quinn saw Lila Vance further down the corridor, her silver sequined dress now smudged with dirt, her usually perfect hair disheveled. She was not filming. Her phone was clutched in her hand like a lifeline, but her eyes, wide and reflecting the flickering emergency lights, were fixed on the swaying walls, her curated composure utterly shattered. For a moment, their eyes met, a brief flicker of shared bewilderment before Lila turned away, pressing herself against the wall as if seeking solace from the cold metal.

The train gave a particularly violent lurch, accompanied by a screech that set Quinn's teeth on edge. Someone screamed. The floor beneath her feet seemed to drop, then slam upwards. It was a sickening, stomach-churning motion. The labored clack-clack of the wheels grew more erratic, more desperate.

Quinn knew, with a certainty that settled like ice in her veins, that this precarious journey could not last. The train was dying.

She braced herself, gripping the doorframe. The lights flickered wildly, then extinguished altogether, plunging them into absolute, terrifying blackness. Only the faint, ghostly green of the emergency exit signs offered any illumination. The grinding, tearing sounds intensified, building to a deafening crescendo.

Then came the fall.

It was not a gradual descent. It was a cataclysmic, instantaneous surrender to gravity and momentum. One moment, Quinn was standing, braced; the next, the world tilted beyond recovery. The carriage she was in seemed to leap sideways, then plunge downwards with unimaginable force. Her scream was lost in the symphony of destruction – the tortured shriek of twisting steel, the explosive shattering of glass, the roar of displaced earth and snow.

She was thrown, not forward, but violently to the side, her body slamming against the opposite wall of the corridor with bone-jarring impact. Air rushed from her lungs. Pain, white-hot and blinding, seared through her shoulder and ribs. The sensation of falling continued, a horrifying, weightless eternity, punctuated by further impacts as the carriage tumbled, rolled, and tore itself apart. Darkness, screams, the smell of diesel fuel and something else, something acrid and burning.

And then, stillness. A ringing, absolute stillness that was somehow more terrifying than the preceding chaos.

Quinn lay amidst a tangle of debris, her cheek pressed against something cold and wet. Snow. The side of the carriage had been ripped open, exposing them to the frigid

Alaskan night. The air was knife-sharp, biting at her exposed skin. She tasted blood, metallic and warm, in her mouth.

Slowly, painfully, she tried to move. Her left arm was a blaze of agony, her shoulder screaming in protest. She pushed herself up with her right arm, her vision swimming. Around her, in the dim, snow-reflected light filtering through the jagged tear in the carriage wall, was a scene of utter devastation. Seats were torn from their moorings, luggage spewed across the wreckage, twisted metal and shattered glass everywhere.

Groans and cries for help rose from the darkness. The air was thick with the smell of fear and spilled fuel.

"Is anyone… is anyone okay?" Quinn managed to call out, her voice raspy.

A weak voice answered nearby. "Help me… I can't move my legs."

The next hour was a blur of desperate effort and mounting horror. Quinn, ignoring the throbbing pain in her shoulder, joined the few other able-bodied survivors and crew members in a frantic attempt to locate and assist the injured. The Aurora Sleeper car, along with at least two others, had been torn from the main body of the train and lay on its side, half-buried in a deep snowdrift at the bottom of a steep, wooded embankment. The angle of the wreckage made movement treacherous. Every shift of weight threatened to send more debris cascading down.

They found Eleanor Ainsworth, the General Manager, near what had once been the observation car's dome. She had a nasty gash on her forehead, blood matting her silver hair, but she was lucid, already trying to organize a response, her voice tight with shock but firm. Alistair Prichard was nearby, surprisingly unscathed but visibly shaken, his expensive suit torn and stained, his usual air of command replaced by a stunned, almost childlike disbelief.

The injuries were horrific. Crushed limbs, deep lacerations, suspected internal bleeding. Bruno, the chef, had a compound fracture in his leg, his face a mask of agony, though he bore it with a stoic, tight-lipped silence. Several passengers were unconscious. The influencers Quinn had seen earlier were a mess of tears and terror; one of them, the young man with the aggressively blond hair, was screaming about his phone, his voice cracking with hysteria, until someone slapped him, hard. It was Lila Vance, her face streaked with grime and tears, her eyes blazing with a desperate fury.

"Shut up!" she shrieked. "People are hurt! Your phone doesn't matter!" The outburst seemed to shock even herself. She then crumpled slightly, her bravado fading, and began to help a crew member bind a wound on an elderly woman's arm.

Quinn helped pull a man free from beneath a heavy piece of paneling. His leg was twisted at an unnatural angle, and he was barely conscious, moaning softly. They did what they could, using torn strips of linen from the sleeper car beds as makeshift bandages, bracing broken limbs with pieces of wreckage. The cold was a relentless enemy, seeping into their bones, making fingers numb and clumsy.

As the bruised dawn finally began to paint the eastern sky in shades of grey and reluctant pink, the true extent of the devastation became clearer. The Borealis Express was a mangled ruin, a silver serpent broken and scattered across the unforgiving landscape. Several cars were still on the tracks, tilted precariously but upright. Others, like theirs, had plunged down the embankment. The engine itself was further up the line, hidden by a curve, but a plume of black smoke rising into the still morning air spoke of its fiery demise.

And then they saw what had caused it.

Hammond, the chief engineer, his face grim and etched with exhaustion, had organized a small party to inspect the tracks uphill from where the first cars had left the rails. Quinn, her shoulder now throbbing with a vengeance but unwilling to remain idle, had joined them, along with a shaken but resolute Alistair Prichard and a few crew members.

They didn't have to go far. About a hundred yards from the point of derailment, where the pristine snow was scarred by the gouges of tortured steel, they found them.

Massive tree trunks. Not one, but three, laid deliberately and with brutal precision across the rails. These were not fallen trees, victims of wind or age. Their bases were crudely hacked, not sawn, the wood splintered and fresh. They were enormous, old-growth timbers that would have taken immense effort to fell and move. They had been placed there. An ambush. A deliberate act of sabotage.

A stunned silence fell over the small group. Alistair Prichard stared at the logs, his face paling, the implications dawning. This was not an accident. This was an attack.

"Who... who would do this?" he whispered, his voice hoarse.

Hammond knelt, examining the closest log. "No ordinary loggers, that's for sure. This is... methodical." He looked up, his gaze sweeping the dense, silent forest that pressed in on them from all sides. The trees stood like silent, watchful sentinels. "Someone didn't want this train to pass."

The elder's words came back to Quinn with chilling force: *Paths that are not asked for are seldom welcome for long. The land remembers.*

The discovery of the logs cast a pall of dread over the survivors. The immediate, frantic need to tend to the injured gave way to a deeper, more insidious fear. They were not just victims of a tragic accident; they were targets.

Attempts to communicate with the outside world proved futile. The train's sophisticated satellite communication system was obliterated. Personal cell phones, as expected in this remote region, showed no signal. The emergency radio in the engine, Hammond reported after a perilous trek to its wreckage, was a molten ruin. They were utterly, terrifyingly alone.

The cold, which had been a persistent discomfort, now became a tangible threat. As the sun climbed higher, it offered little warmth. The temperature hovered well below freezing, and a biting wind swept down from the mountains, cutting through their inadequate clothing. Those who had been in their nightclothes or party attire suffered the most. Shivering became a constant, involuntary chorus. Hypothermia was a very real danger.

Eleanor Ainsworth, despite her own injury, tried to maintain a semblance of order. She organized a headcount, her voice trembling slightly as she called out names from the passenger manifest. The process was grim. Several people were unresponsive, their injuries too severe. Others were simply gone, their absence a chilling testament to the violence of the derailment.

Then came the discrepancy.

"Mr. David Ackroyd?" Eleanor called out, her brow furrowed. "Is Mr. David Ackroyd present?"

Silence. She called the name again, louder this time. No response.

"Does anyone know Mr. Ackroyd? Has anyone seen him?"

A few people shook their heads. The name meant nothing to most. Quinn vaguely recalled a quiet, middle-aged man who had kept to himself in the observation car, reading a book.

"He was in car seven," a crew member offered. "The one just behind the main dining car. It's... it's one of the worst."

A quick, grim search of the mangled remains of car seven yielded no sign of David Ackroyd. He wasn't among the injured, nor, as far as they could tell in the chaotic wreckage, among the dead they had managed to identify. He was simply missing. Vanished.

The news rippled through the survivors, adding another layer of unease. Had he been thrown clear? Wandered off in a daze? Or had something else happened to him? The thought, unspoken but palpable, hung in the frigid air: had he been taken? Taken by whatever, or whoever, had placed those logs on the track?

The day wore on, a grim tableau of suffering and fear. The seriously injured were made as comfortable as possible in one ofr the less damaged, though still tilted, carriages. Those who could move scavenged for anything useful: blankets, water bottles, first-aid kits, food from the ravaged dining car. The opulence of The Borealis Express was now a cruel joke, its gourmet provisions scattered and frozen, its fine linens stained with blood.

Alistair Prichard, after his initial shock, seemed to retreat into himself. He sat alone, staring blankly at the wreckage, the architect of this grand, failed venture now just another cold, frightened survivor. The influencers, stripped of their audience and their props, huddled together for warmth, their usual ebullience extinguished. Lila Vance, surprisingly, proved to be one of the more resilient, her earlier outburst seemingly a catalyst. She worked tirelessly, helping the injured, her movements practical, her face set in a grim mask of determination. Quinn found a grudging respect for her. Trauma, it seemed, was a great leveler.

As late afternoon approached, casting long, ominous shadows across the snow, Hammond made a decision. He was a man of action, an engineer accustomed to solving problems, and the helplessness of their situation clearly weighed heavily on him.

"I'm going to scout ahead," he announced to Eleanor and a small group that included Quinn and Prichard. "Follow the line. There might be a ranger station, an old logging camp, something. Or I can try to walk back towards the last signal point. We can't just sit here and wait to freeze."

Eleanor protested. "Hammond, it's too dangerous. We don't know what's out there. Those logs…"

"Those logs are exactly why I have to go," Hammond countered, his jaw set. "Someone put them there. If they're still around…" He didn't finish the sentence, but his meaning was clear. "Besides, if there's any chance of getting help, we have to take it. I know this terrain better than anyone else here. I'll take a radio, what's left of one, and a flare gun."

He was referring to a couple of short-range walkie-talkies they had salvaged, their range pitifully limited, and a single emergency flare gun with only three cartridges found in a locker.

No amount of argument could sway him. He was a man driven by a sense of duty, perhaps also by a need to escape the suffocating atmosphere of the wreck site. He gathered a few meager supplies: a bottle of water, some salvaged protein bars, an extra jacket. He checked the battered flare gun, his movements precise and economical.

Quinn watched him, a knot of apprehension tightening in her stomach. He was a capable man, strong and experienced. But the wilderness felt different now, imbued with a malevolence that went beyond its natural dangers. The forest seemed to watch them, its silence no longer peaceful but predatory.

Before he left, Hammond approached Quinn. "Mallory," he said, his voice low. "You know a bit about these woods, right? Your essay."

Quinn nodded, surprised.

"If I'm not back by… say, midday tomorrow, or if you don't hear from me on the radio by nightfall… don't come looking." His eyes were serious. "Get these people to fortify this position as best they can. Stay together. And keep an eye on those trees."

He didn't elaborate. He didn't need to.

With a final, grim nod to the remaining group, Hammond shouldered his small pack and set off, following the scarred path of the railway line as it curved out of sight into the dense, snow-laden spruce and pine. He walked with a steady, determined gait, a small, solitary figure against the vast, indifferent wilderness.

The survivors watched him go until he was swallowed by the trees. A profound silence descended, broken only by the mournful sigh of the wind through the skeletal branches and the distant, unsettling caw of a raven.

As the light began to fade, and the temperature dropped even further, the remaining passengers and crew huddled together in the least damaged carriages, the fear a palpable entity among them. Hammond was gone. Communications were dead. The cold was relentless. And out there, in the deepening shadows of the Alaskan wilderness, something had deliberately, violently, broken the line. Something that, Quinn suspected with a certainty that made her shiver, was still watching.

Chapter 3 – No One's Coming

The second night descended upon the mangled remains of The Borealis Express like a physical weight, a suffocating blanket of cold and impenetrable darkness. The brief respite offered by the pale Alaskan sun had vanished, and with it, any lingering vestiges of hope for a swift rescue. Hammond had not returned. The walkie-talkies remained stubbornly silent, their occasional crackle of static only emphasizing the vast, empty wilderness that surrounded them. No distant thrum of helicopter blades broke the profound stillness, no searchlights pierced the oppressive gloom. The realization settled upon the survivors with the chilling finality of a death sentence: no one was coming. Not tonight. Perhaps not ever.

Panic, a cold, insidious serpent, began to uncoil in the bellies of even the most stoic. It manifested in different ways. Some, like Alistair Prichard, retreated into a stony, shocked silence, his gaze fixed on the flickering flames of the pitiful fire they had managed to build in a cleared area near the least damaged carriage. The fire, fed with splintered wood from the wreckage and a few drier branches scavenged from the forest edge, offered more psychological comfort than actual warmth against the biting, sub-zero air. Prichard, the visionary billionaire, now looked like a broken old man, his bespoke suit a mockery in this theatre of primal fear.

Others succumbed to a jittery, restless anxiety. They paced, they muttered, they jumped at every snap of a twig from the encroaching forest. The young man with the aggressively blond hair, whose name Quinn learned was Chad, had thankfully stopped wailing about his phone after Lila's fierce rebuke. Now, he sat huddled with the two other influencers, a woman named Tiffany who was weeping softly into a cashmere scarf, and another, Kendal, who stared blankly ahead, her meticulously applied makeup now smudged and grotesque in the firelight.

Eleanor Ainsworth, her face pale but resolute beneath the bloodstained bandage on her forehead, moved among the survivors, offering what little comfort she could. Her voice, though strained, remained a beacon of attempted order. "We need to conserve our energy," she urged, her breath pluming in the frigid air. "Stay warm. Try to rest." But rest was an elusive luxury when every shadow seemed to menace and every gust of wind through the skeletal trees sounded like a whispered threat.

Quinn found herself gravitating towards the periphery of the small, miserable encampment. The throbbing in her shoulder had subsided to a dull, persistent ache, a constant reminder of the violence of the derailment. She had managed to salvage her outdoor gear from her duffel bag – thermal layers, a waterproof jacket, sturdy gloves, and a warm hat. Dressed in these, she felt marginally more prepared than those still shivering in their evening wear, but the cold was a pervasive, insidious enemy, seeping through every layer.

She watched the forest, her gaze sweeping the black, impenetrable wall of trees that ringed their precarious sanctuary. Hammond's parting words echoed in her mind:

Keep an eye on those trees. It was advice she took to heart. The forest did not feel empty. It felt watchful, alive with a silent, unseen presence. The hairs on the back of her neck prickled, an primal instinct she had learned to trust during her time in wild places.

Lila Vance, surprisingly, seemed to be channeling her fear into a strange, almost manic energy. After her earlier display of unexpected fortitude, she had retrieved her primary vlogging camera from her miraculously intact designer luggage. The small, professional-grade device, with its articulated screen and external microphone, looked absurdly out of place in this scene of raw survival.

"Okay, guys," Lila said, her voice a little too bright, a little too forced, as she addressed the camera lens. Chad and Kendal looked up, their expressions a mixture of confusion and faint, reflexive interest. Tiffany continued to sob. "So, like, total plot twist. The Borealis Express? Not so express anymore." She attempted a wry smile that didn't quite land. "We're, um, experiencing some technical difficulties. Major ones. But your girl Lila is here, bringing you the exclusive. This is, like, extreme wilderness survival. Hashtag Unfiltered. Hashtag AlaskaChallenge."

Quinn stared, astonished at the woman's disconnect. Was she truly this oblivious, or was this a bizarre coping mechanism, a retreat into the only reality she understood?

"Lila, what in God's name are you doing?" Eleanor's voice was sharp, cutting through Lila's forced monologue.

Lila lowered the camera slightly, a flicker of defiance in her eyes. "I'm documenting, Eleanor. This is… this is content. People will want to see this. It's real."

"Real?" A harsh laugh escaped one of the crew members, a grizzled man named Marcus whose hand was crudely bandaged. "Lady, people are hurt. People might be dying. Hammond is out there, God knows where. And you're worried about content?"

"It's not just content," Lila insisted, though her voice wavered. "It's… it's a record. What if… what if no one finds us? This could be all that's left." The bravado in her voice cracked, revealing a sliver of the terror beneath.

Before anyone else could respond, a new sound cut through the night, silencing all argument. It was a high-pitched whine, unnatural and jarring against the organic sounds of the wilderness.

All heads turned towards its source. One of the tech crew, a young man named Ben, was hunched over a small, sophisticated drone he had managed to salvage from the wreckage of the crew car. He had been working on it for hours, his face illuminated by the glow of a connected tablet.

"Got it!" Ben exclaimed, a note of triumph in his voice. "Battery's low, and the gimbal's a bit sticky, but it's flying. Maybe we can get a signal out, or at least see what's around us."

A fragile tendril of hope sprouted amidst the despair. A drone. It was a small chance, but it was something.

The drone, a sleek, black quadcopter, whirred to life, its small rotors spinning rapidly. With a practiced touch, Ben sent it ascending into the black sky. Its small navigation lights blinked, red and green, like malevolent fireflies against the star-dusted canvas. On the tablet, a grainy, black-and-white image appeared – the drone's view of their pathetic encampment, the flickering fire a small orange blotch in a sea of darkness.

"Taking it up," Ben murmured, his brow furrowed in concentration. "Trying to get some altitude. See if I can pick up any cell towers on the peaks, though it's a long shot."

The drone climbed higher, its whining sound fading slightly. The image on the tablet shifted, showing the tops of the trees, a dark, textured carpet stretching out in all directions. Then, mountains, their jagged silhouettes stark against the night sky. No lights. No signs of civilization. Just an endless expanse of wilderness.

Lila, her earlier project momentarily forgotten, had moved closer, her camera now pointed at the tablet screen, capturing Ben's attempt. Even in this dire situation, the instinct to film was deeply ingrained.

"Anything?" Quinn asked, her voice low.

Ben shook his head, his eyes glued to the screen. "Nothing yet. Just… trees. Lots of trees." He manipulated the controls, panning the drone's camera slowly. "Range is limited with this damage. And the wind's picking up at altitude."

The image on the tablet suddenly jittered, then filled with static for a horrifying second. Ben swore under his breath, his knuckles white as he gripped the controls. "Losing signal… come on, come on…"

The image flickered back, clearer this time, but something was different. The drone was lower, much lower, as if it had been buffeted downwards. It was now skimming just above the treetops, a mile or so from their camp, the image jerky and unstable.

"What happened?" Eleanor asked, her voice tight.

"Sudden downdraft, I think," Ben said, though he sounded uncertain. "Or maybe interference. It's fighting me."

And then, they saw it. Or thought they saw it.

For a fraction of a second, a shape moved in the drone's field of vision. It was at the edge of the frame, between two towering spruce trees, a fleeting silhouette against the snow. It was large, upright, and moved with an unnatural, fluid speed that defied easy categorization. Too big for a deer, too agile for a bear. It was there, then it was gone, vanishing into the blackness between the trees as if swallowed by the shadows themselves.

"What was that?" Chad whispered, his voice cracking.

Ben stared at the screen, his face pale. "I… I don't know. An animal? A moose?"

"It didn't move like a moose," Quinn said, her heart suddenly hammering. The image, brief and indistinct as it was, had sent a jolt of pure, primal fear through her. It was the way it moved – purposeful, swift, almost… intelligent.

"Rewind it," Alistair Prichard commanded, his voice raspy but firm, his earlier apathy momentarily broken. "Let me see that again."

Ben fumbled with the controls. "It's live feed, Mr. Prichard. I can't rewind. But I'm recording." He tried to pan the drone back towards the spot, but the image was becoming increasingly unstable, filled with glitches and interference. "Damn it, I'm losing control. It's not responding."

The drone's whining motor sound, which had been a distant hum, suddenly pitched higher, then cut out with an abrupt, sickening silence. On the tablet, the image froze on a chaotic blur of snow and branches, then went black.

"No!" Ben cried out, slapping the side of the tablet. "Signal lost. It's down. The drone is down."

A heavy silence fell over the group, broken only by Tiffany's renewed, frightened sobs. The brief flicker of hope the drone had offered was extinguished, replaced by a new, more specific dread. That fleeting image, that dark, swift shape in the woods, replayed in Quinn's mind. It was barely visible, grainy, inconclusive – the kind of thing easily dismissed as a trick of light, a shadow, an overactive imagination.

But Quinn knew what she had seen. Or rather, what she had *felt* when she saw it. It was the same feeling the elder's warning had evoked. The same feeling she got when she looked into the deep, watchful woods.

Lila, surprisingly, was the one who voiced it. Her camera was still recording, though her hand was shaking. "That… that wasn't an animal," she said, her voice barely a whisper. "That was… something else." Her eyes, wide and terrified, met Quinn's. The curated persona was gone, replaced by raw, unfiltered fear.

The night deepened. The fire dwindled, despite their efforts to feed it. The cold intensified, gnawing at them, making their teeth chatter and their limbs ache. Sleep was impossible. Every snap of a twig, every rustle of leaves in the wind, sent fresh waves of anxiety through the huddled survivors.

And then came the vocalizations.

It started subtly, a sound so strange and distant that at first, Quinn thought she was imagining it, a product of her frayed nerves and the wind sighing through the pines. But then it came again, closer this time, and others heard it too.

It was not the howl of a wolf, nor the growl of a bear. It was not the cry of any known animal. It was a long, ululating call, a sound that seemed to rise from the very depths of the earth, filled with a primal sorrow and an unearthly menace. It echoed through the silent forest, a mournful, chilling serenade that seemed to penetrate their very bones.

Then came other sounds. A series of guttural clicks and whistles, too complex for a mere beast. A low, rumbling sound, like distant thunder, yet there were no clouds in the star-dusted sky. And then, most terrifying of all, a sound that was almost like laughter — a harsh, barking sound that held no mirth, only a chilling, predatory intelligence.

The survivors huddled closer together, their faces pale masks of terror in the dying firelight. Alistair Prichard, the billionaire, was visibly trembling, his eyes wide with a fear that transcended any financial loss. Eleanor Ainsworth clutched a heavy wrench she had salvaged from the wreckage, her knuckles white. Bruno, the injured chef, propped himself up on his good arm, his face grim, listening intently. Even the influencers were silent, their fear too profound for words or cameras.

The sounds seemed to circle their camp, sometimes distant, sometimes alarmingly close. They were never identifiable, never attributable to any creature Quinn knew from her extensive knowledge of Alaskan wildlife. These were the sounds of something other, something ancient and unknown, something that was now aware of their presence and, it seemed, was toying with them.

Quinn felt a cold dread settle deep within her. These were not random animal noises. There was a pattern to them, a call and response, a terrifying suggestion of communication. The forest, which had seemed merely indifferent, now felt actively hostile, alive with unseen watchers.

As the first, faint hint of dawn began to stain the eastern sky, a bruised purple that offered little promise of warmth or rescue, Quinn knew she had to do something more than just listen and wait. The sounds had receded with the approaching light, but the sense of being watched remained, stronger than ever.

She moved away from the dying fire, her movements slow and deliberate, trying not to draw attention. She circled the perimeter of their small, wrecked sanctuary, her eyes scanning the snow-covered ground at the edge of the forest. The fresh snowfall from the previous day had been light, but it was enough.

And there, she found them.

Subtle signs, easily missed by an untrained eye, but to Quinn, they screamed a silent warning. A series of indentations in the snow, just beyond the reach of the firelight, partially obscured by wind-drift. They were huge, elongated, too large for any bear. The stride was immense. And there was something else – a faint, almost imperceptible drag mark between some of the prints, as if something heavy had been pulled.

Further along, she found a small spruce tree, one of its lower branches snapped cleanly, not broken by wind or snow load, but twisted off with considerable force. The raw, splintered wood was fresh. And beneath it, almost hidden in the snow, a single, dark strand of hair – long, coarse, and unlike anything she had ever seen. It was not animal fur.

She continued her circuit, her heart pounding a slow, heavy rhythm against her ribs. More signs. A peculiar arrangement of stones on a fallen log, too deliberate to be natural. A patch of snow that seemed to have been smoothed over, as if to erase tracks. And then, the most chilling discovery of all: near the base of a massive, ancient cedar, almost invisible against the dark bark, was a carving. It was fresh, the pale wood beneath exposed. It was not a symbol she recognized, but it was undeniably a mark, a territorial sign, etched with a crude but powerful hand.

They were being watched. Tracked. Herded, perhaps. The logs on the railway line were not an isolated act of sabotage. They were a declaration. The drone had not simply malfunctioned; it had been brought down, or lured. The vocalizations were not random; they were communication, a taunt, a warning.

Quinn returned to the group, her face grim. The others were stirring, stiff and cold, their faces etched with exhaustion and fear. Eleanor was trying to rally them, talking about rationing the remaining food, about trying to signal for help again when the sun was fully up.

Quinn waited for a lull, then spoke, her voice low but clear, carrying a weight that made everyone turn to look at her.

"Hammond was right," she said, her gaze sweeping over their pale, frightened faces. "We're not alone out here. And whatever it is, it knows we're here. It's been watching us all night." She held up the coarse strand of hair. "It's tracking us."

The fragile hope that had flickered with the dawn died a swift, brutal death. The truth, stark and terrifying, settled upon them. No one was coming. And something else, something ancient and malevolent, was already here, its presence now as undeniable as the biting cold and the vast, indifferent wilderness that held them captive. The line had been broken, and they were on the wrong side of it.

Chapter 4 – Branches Like Bones

Quinn's words, stark and devoid of comforting platitudes, fell into the frigid morning air like stones into a deep, dark well. The coarse strand of hair she held aloft, a tangible piece of evidence, seemed to suck the last vestiges of warmth from their pathetic encampment. For a long moment, no one spoke. The only sounds were the mournful sigh of the wind through the skeletal branches of the surrounding forest and the distant, unsettling caw of a raven, a sound that now seemed laden with ominous portent.

Then, denial, that fragile human shield against unbearable truths, began to crumble.

"Tracking us?" Chad, the influencer, whispered, his voice hoarse. His aggressively blond hair was matted, his face, usually a canvas for carefully curated expressions of ironic detachment, was now a mask of raw, unadulterated terror. "What do you mean, tracking us? Like… an animal?"

"The prints I found were not made by any animal I know," Quinn stated, her gaze steady, though her insides churned with a cold dread. "They were bipedal. Huge. And the branch that was snapped, the carving on the cedar… this is intelligent. Territorial."

Alistair Prichard, who had been a picture of broken apathy, straightened slightly. A flicker of his old imperious self returned, though it was weak, like a dying ember. "Nonsense. It's… it must be a bear. A very large, very unusual bear. Or perhaps… perhaps some local hermit, a madman living in these woods, trying to scare us." Even as he spoke, the words sounded hollow, unconvincing.

"A hermit who can fell three massive trees and place them across railway tracks with surgical precision?" Marcus, the grizzled crewman with the bandaged hand, scoffed. His face was grim. "A hermit who can make those sounds we heard last night? Sounds that weren't human and weren't any beast I've ever encountered in thirty years of working these lines?"

Eleanor Ainsworth, her face etched with worry, looked at Quinn. "The hair, Quinn… are you certain?"

Quinn nodded. "It's not bear fur. It's not moose, not caribou. It's… different." She didn't want to say 'humanoid', but the implication hung heavy in the air.

The group fell silent again, the weight of their predicament pressing down on them. They were stranded, injured, with dwindling supplies and no hope of immediate rescue. And now, they knew, definitively, that they were not alone. They were being stalked by something unknown, something powerful, something that had already demonstrated its capacity for destructive, calculated violence.

It was Bruno, the Michelin-starred chef, his leg crudely splinted and propped up on a pile of salvaged seat cushions, who broke the silence. His usually florid face was pale with pain and exhaustion, but his dark eyes burned with a fierce, almost feral intensity.

"So," Bruno said, his voice a low growl, his Italian accent thick. "We are hunted. Bene. This changes things." He gestured with his good hand towards the wreckage of the dining car. "There are knives in there. Cleavers. Steel pans that can break a skull. If it comes for us, it will not find sheep."

His words, brutal and direct, seemed to galvanize some of the survivors. A spark of defiance, however small, flickered in the face of overwhelming fear. Others, however, seemed to shrink further into themselves, their terror deepening. Tiffany, one of the influencers, began to weep again, her sobs muffled by her expensive scarf.

The morning wore on, a grim exercise in trying to impose order on chaos. They took a more thorough inventory of their meager supplies: a few bottles of water, some scattered packages of airline snacks, a couple of half-empty first-aid kits. The gourmet provisions of the dining car were mostly unusable, frozen solid or contaminated by diesel fuel. The cold remained their most immediate and relentless enemy.

The debate about what to do began in hushed, fearful whispers, then grew into a more open, desperate discussion. Staying put meant conserving energy, but it also meant remaining a fixed target, waiting for the unseen entity to make its next move. Leaving meant facing the perils of the wilderness, the brutal cold, and the unknown dangers of the forest, but it offered a sliver of hope, however faint, of finding shelter, or help, or at least a more defensible position.

"We have to try to move," Ben, the young tech crew member who had operated the drone, argued. His face was drawn, his eyes haunted by the memory of the fleeting figure on his tablet screen. "We can't just sit here. What if it… what if it comes back for the rest of us?"

"And go where?" Alistair Prichard countered, his voice regaining some of its former sharpness, though it was laced with an unfamiliar tremor of fear. "Wander into that forest? With the injured? With no idea where we're going? That's suicide."

"Staying here is suicide!" a passenger, a middle-aged woman whose name Quinn didn't know, cried out. "Didn't you hear those things last night? Didn't you see what Quinn found?"

Eleanor Ainsworth tried to mediate, her voice calm but strained. "We need a plan. A rational plan. Rushing into the wilderness without supplies or a clear destination is not the answer. But neither is… waiting."

It was Quinn who finally proposed the compromise, born of a desperate pragmatism. "We split up," she said, her voice cutting through the rising tide of panicked debate.

All eyes turned to her.

"Some of us stay here," Quinn continued, choosing her words carefully. "With the wreckage. It offers some shelter, however minimal. And if, by some miracle, a rescue team does come looking, this is where they'll search first. We fortify this position as best we can. Bruno is right; we gather whatever can be used as weapons."

She paused, then looked towards the silent, watching forest. "And some of us try to walk out. A small group. Fast-moving. We follow the railway line, like Hammond was trying to do. Or we try to reach higher ground, see if we can get a signal. It's a slim chance, but it's better than doing nothing."

The proposal was met with a mixture of reactions. Some saw it as a death sentence for whichever group they weren't in. Others grasped at it as the only viable option, a way to take some form of action, however desperate.

"And who decides who goes and who stays?" Prichard demanded, his eyes narrowed.

"Those who are too injured to travel must stay," Quinn said, her gaze resting for a moment on Bruno, and on an elderly man who was clearly suffering from severe hypothermia. "We need volunteers for the trek. People who are fit, who have some experience, or at least the will to survive."

Lila Vance, who had been surprisingly quiet, her camera dangling forgotten from her wrist, suddenly spoke up. "I'll go."

All heads turned to her, surprise evident on many faces. Lila, the image-obsessed influencer, volunteering for a perilous trek through the Alaskan wilderness?

"Lila, are you sure?" Eleanor asked, her brow furrowed with concern.

Lila nodded, a new, unfamiliar hardness in her eyes. The curated facade had been stripped away by terror and trauma, revealing something stronger, something more resilient beneath. "I can't just sit here," she said, her voice surprisingly firm. "I have to… do something. And I still have my camera. If we see anything… if we find anything… the world needs to know." Her old motivations, twisted and reshaped by their current nightmare, still flickered.

Quinn looked at Lila, a flicker of grudging respect in her eyes. Perhaps the woman had more substance than she had given her credit for. "Alright, Lila. You're in."

Ben, the drone operator, also volunteered, along with Marcus, the grizzled crewman, and a quiet, athletic-looking young woman who had been a passenger, an architect named Sarah. That made five of them: Quinn, Lila, Ben, Marcus, and Sarah. A small, reasonably able-bodied group.

The decision, once made, cast a fresh pall over the survivors. The act of splitting, of deliberately separating, felt like an admission of defeat, a tacit acknowledgment that their chances of survival as a whole group were slim. Goodbyes were subdued, fraught with unspoken fears. Those who were staying watched with a mixture of envy and terror as the small trek group made their preparations.

They gathered what little they could: a shared blanket, a few bottles of water, the last of the protein bars, the single flare gun with its three precious cartridges, and a couple of heavy-duty flashlights with fading batteries. Bruno, despite his injury, insisted on giving Marcus one of his sharpest boning knives. "You see that *bastardo*," he growled, his eyes glinting, "you put this in its eye."

Quinn took charge of the small map of the rail line she had found in Hammond's discarded jacket, its route now a cruel mockery of their intended journey. She also carried the small, potent canister of bear spray she always had in her pack – a last resort, but perhaps a useful one.

As the trek group prepared to depart, those remaining behind began, with a grim determination, to fortify their position. Under Eleanor's direction, they dragged heavier pieces of wreckage to create a crude barricade around the least damaged carriage, the one where the most seriously injured were housed. They sharpened pieces of metal, fashioned clubs from broken seat legs. The atmosphere was one of desperate, fearful resolve.

Before leaving, Quinn took one last look around the encampment. Alistair Prichard was staring into the fire, his face a mask of despair. Chad and Kendal were huddled together, their faces pale and drawn. Tiffany was still weeping. Eleanor was trying to comfort the elderly man, whose breathing was shallow and ragged. It was a scene of profound human misery, a stark testament to the brutal indifference of the wilderness and the malevolent intelligence that stalked them.

"Good luck, Quinn," Eleanor said, her voice thick with emotion. She gripped Quinn's arm, her eyes filled with a mixture of hope and fear. "Find help. Please."

Quinn nodded, unable to speak past the lump in her throat. She knew the chances were slim. But they had to try.

With a final, grim nod to the others, the small trek group set off, following the mangled railway line into the oppressive silence of the forest. The snow crunched under their boots, the sound unnaturally loud in the stillness. The trees, laden with snow, seemed to press in on them, their branches like skeletal arms, their dense foliage swallowing the light.

The going was brutal. The railway sleepers were uneven, often dislodged, and the ballast was treacherous underfoot. They moved slowly, conserving their energy, acutely aware of every sound, every shadow. The forest was unnervingly silent. No birdsong, no rustle of small animals. Just the sigh of the wind and the crunch of their own footsteps.

Lila, surprisingly, kept pace, her earlier fragility replaced by a grim determination. She filmed intermittently, her commentary sparse, her voice hushed, capturing the desolation of their surroundings, the fear in her companions' eyes. It was no longer about likes or followers; it was about bearing witness.

After an hour of arduous trekking, Marcus, who was in the lead, suddenly stopped, holding up a hand. "Wait," he whispered, his eyes narrowed, scanning the trees ahead. "Do you smell that?"

Quinn sniffed the air. A faint, acrid scent, like something burning, but with an underlying, deeply unpleasant organic odor. It was carried on the wind, elusive but undeniable.

"Smoke?" Ben asked, his voice barely audible.

"Not just smoke," Quinn said, her senses on high alert. "Something else. Something… rotten."

They proceeded with extreme caution, moving from tree to tree, their makeshift weapons held ready. The smell grew stronger, thicker, making their stomachs churn.

And then they saw it.

In a small clearing, a short distance from the tracks, was a sight that froze them in their tracks, a grotesque tableau of primitive ritual and unimaginable savagery.

A crude totem pole, if it could be called that, had been erected. It was fashioned from a young pine tree, its branches hacked off, its bark stripped away in places. Impaled upon its sharpened top, and hanging from its crudely severed limbs, were the remains of animals. A snowshoe hare, its fur matted with frozen blood. A ptarmigan, its wings spread in a mockery of flight. And, most disturbingly, what looked like the severed head of a young deer, its eyes wide and glassy, staring sightlessly at the sky.

At the base of the totem, a small fire smoldered, the source of the acrid smoke. But it was not wood that burned. It was a pile of bones and fur, crackling and spitting, releasing the nauseating stench that had drawn them closer. The snow around the totem was stained dark, a mixture of ash and what looked like dried blood.

This was no random animal kill. This was a shrine. A warning. A declaration of ownership.

Lila let out a small, choked gasp, her hand flying to her mouth, her camera forgotten. Ben looked like he was going to be sick. Marcus swore, a low, vicious sound. Sarah, the architect, stared at the gruesome display, her face pale but her eyes filled with a horrified understanding.

Quinn felt a cold dread seep into her very marrow. This was beyond anything she could have imagined. The intelligence they were facing was not just predatory; it was ritualistic, possessed of a terrifying, alien understanding of symbolism and fear. The burned animal totem, still smoking in the snow, was a clear message, a brutal assertion of dominance over this territory.

"We need to go," Quinn said, her voice tight, pulling her gaze away from the horrifying shrine. "Now. Before whatever made this comes back."

They retreated, quickly and quietly, their earlier exhaustion forgotten, replaced by a fresh surge of adrenaline-fueled terror. The image of the smoking totem, the impaled animals, the stench of burning bones, was seared into their minds.

Meanwhile, back at the wreckage of The Borealis Express, the remaining survivors faced their own unfolding horror. The day had passed in a blur of fear and anxious waiting. The fortification of the carriage, while offering a sliver of psychological comfort, did little to alleviate the oppressive sense of dread. Every snap of a twig, every shadow that lengthened with the declining sun, sent fresh waves of panic through the huddled group.

Bruno, despite his intense pain, had become the de facto guardian. Propped near the barricaded entrance of the carriage, a heavy meat cleaver resting on his lap, his dark eyes scanned the surrounding forest with unwavering intensity. He had seen things in his life, he had told Eleanor in a low voice, things that made the blood run cold. He recognized the signs of a predator, and he knew, with a chilling certainty, that this predator was unlike any he had ever encountered.

As dusk began to settle, casting the forest in shades of grey and purple, a subtle change began to occur in their immediate surroundings. At first, it was almost imperceptible, easily dismissed as a trick of the fading light or the product of frayed nerves. A low-hanging branch on a nearby spruce seemed to be lower than it had been that morning. A narrow game trail that had been visible at the edge of the clearing now seemed to be obscured by a sudden, dense tangle of new undergrowth.

It was Chad, the influencer, who first voiced the unnerving observation, his voice trembling. "Hey… guys? Does that tree… does it look different to you?" He pointed a shaking finger towards a tall pine just beyond their crude barricade. "I swear… I swear those branches weren't like that before. They look… closer. Like they're reaching."

Eleanor tried to reassure him. "It's just the light, Chad. Your eyes are playing tricks on you." But even as she spoke, she felt a prickle of unease. She, too, had noticed subtle shifts, changes in the familiar landscape around their camp that she couldn't quite explain.

As the darkness deepened, the changes became more undeniable, more menacing. Trees that had seemed distant now loomed closer. Branches that had been bare now seemed to sprout new, thorny offshoots, like skeletal fingers reaching for them. The very fabric of the forest around them seemed to be subtly, malevolently, rearranging itself. Paths that had been clear were now blocked by freshly fallen logs, too large to have been moved by wind alone. The air grew heavy, oppressive, as if the woods themselves were holding their breath.

The stayers huddled deeper into the carriage, the flickering light of their small, salvaged lantern casting long, dancing shadows that writhed like living things. The sense of being watched, of being slowly, inexorably encircled, was overwhelming.

And then, they found Hammond.

It was Alistair Prichard who made the discovery. Driven by a restless, gnawing anxiety, and perhaps a desperate, foolish hope that Hammond might still return, he had ventured a short distance from the carriage, peering into the deepening gloom along the railway line. He carried a heavy iron poker from the wrecked fireplace of the lounge car, his only weapon.

His scream, when it came, was not loud. It was a choked, gurgling sound, a sound of pure, unadulterated horror that cut through the frigid air and brought everyone stumbling out of the carriage, their makeshift weapons clutched in trembling hands.

They found Prichard on his knees in the snow, vomiting, his face a ghastly shade of green in the lantern light. He was pointing a shaking finger towards a massive, ancient spruce tree that stood like a dark sentinel beside the tracks, about fifty yards from their camp.

Hanging from one of its thick lower branches, swaying gently in the cold night breeze, was the body of Hammond, the engineer.

He was not merely dead. He had been... arranged. His body was suspended by his own belt, his head lolling at an unnatural angle. His eyes, wide and staring, reflected the lantern light with a glassy, vacant horror. His uniform was torn, his limbs strangely contorted. And around his neck, fashioned from twisted vines and what looked like strips of his own clothing, was a crude, horrifying parody of a noose.

But it was what was *on* the branches around him that truly broke them. The branches of the spruce tree, the ones immediately surrounding Hammond's suspended body, were not bare. They were festooned, decorated, with bones. Small animal bones, picked clean and bleached white, tied to the needles with strands of what looked like sinew. They hung there like gruesome Christmas ornaments, clicking softly together in the wind, a macabre wind chime accompanying the silent, swaying figure of the dead engineer.

Branches like bones. Bones like branches.

The message was clear, brutal, and unequivocal. This was a warning. A display. A testament to the power and the cruelty of the thing that hunted them.

Eleanor stifled a scream, her hand flying to her mouth. Bruno let out a string of furious, heartbroken Italian curses, his knuckles white as he gripped his cleaver. Even the influencers, Chad and Kendal, stared in stunned, silent horror, their earlier anxieties and self-obsessions obliterated by this visceral, undeniable proof of the nightmare they were trapped in.

Hammond, the capable, pragmatic engineer, the one who had set out with such grim determination to find help, had become a grotesque ornament in the entity's terrifying gallery.

The line had not just been broken. It had become a hunting ground. And they, the survivors of The Borealis Express, were the prey.

Chapter 5 – Red Snow

The retreat from the smoking totem was a silent, panicked flight. Words were unnecessary, dangerous even. Every snap of a twig under their worn boots, every rustle of wind through the dense, snow-laden boughs, sounded like the prelude to an ambush. The gruesome shrine, with its impaled animals and the nauseating stench of burning bones, had stripped away any lingering hope that they were dealing with something rational, something that could be understood or appeased. This was an entity of primal rage and terrifying, ritualistic intelligence.

Quinn led the small group, pushing them onward, away from the railway line now. The tracks, which had once seemed a tenuous link to civilization, now felt like an exposed artery, a clear path for whatever hunted them. She veered them deeper into the forest, seeking the relative cover of thicker stands of spruce and fir, though the oppressive silence of the woods offered little comfort. The trees themselves felt like silent, judging witnesses, their ancient forms unmoved by the fleeting terrors of human lives.

Marcus, the grizzled crewman, his face a mask of grim fury, brought up the rear, Bruno's boning knife clutched tightly in his hand. Ben, the young tech, stumbled frequently, his eyes wide and darting, his earlier confidence completely shattered. Sarah, the architect, moved with a quiet, focused determination, her gaze constantly scanning their surroundings, though her pale face betrayed the terror she undoubtedly felt.

Lila Vance was a revelation. The influencer, stripped of her audience and her carefully constructed persona, had found a core of unexpected steel. She still carried her camera, but it was no longer an extension of her vanity. It was a tool, a silent witness. She filmed in short, jerky bursts, her breath misting in the frigid air, her lens capturing the fear etched on her companions' faces, the oppressive gloom of the forest, the blood-red berries on a lonely holly bush that seemed to mock their plight. There was no commentary now, no hashtags, just the raw, unfiltered reality of their desperate flight.

They pushed themselves relentlessly, driven by a primal fear that transcended exhaustion and the gnawing ache of hunger. The terrain grew more difficult as they moved away from the relatively flat ground of the railway embankment. They scrambled over fallen logs, pushed through dense thickets of alder, their progress slow and agonizing. The cold was a constant, biting companion, seeping through their layers, numbing their extremities.

Quinn estimated they had been moving for another two hours since fleeing the totem when she called for a brief halt. They were in a small, relatively sheltered hollow, surrounded by a ring of ancient, moss-covered boulders. "We need to rest," she said, her voice low, her breath pluming. "Just for a few minutes. Conserve energy. Drink some water if you have any left."

They collapsed onto the cold, damp ground, their chests heaving, their faces slick with sweat despite the freezing temperatures. Ben fumbled with his water bottle, his hands shaking so badly he could barely unscrew the cap. Marcus leaned against a boulder, his eyes scanning their back trail, his expression unreadable.

"How much further, Quinn?" Sarah asked, her voice barely a whisper. "Do you… do you think we're putting any distance between us and… that?"

Quinn consulted the tattered map, though it was of little use now that they were off the marked railway line. "I don't know," she admitted, the honesty costing her. "We're heading roughly west, trying to parallel the line but stay hidden. If there's a ranger station, or any kind of outpost, it would likely be marked on this map, but we're in uncharted territory here." She folded the map, the paper crinkling loudly in the stillness. "Our best hope is to find a ridge, get some elevation. Maybe Ben can try to get a signal then."

Ben looked up, his eyes hollow. "My phone's almost dead. And after what happened to the drone…" He didn't need to finish the sentence. The hope of electronic salvation felt impossibly remote.

It was during this brief, uneasy respite that it happened.

Marcus, ever vigilant, had risen to his feet, peering through a narrow gap in the boulders. "Thought I saw something," he muttered, more to himself than to the others. "Just a flicker. Probably my eyes playing tricks." He took a few steps out of the hollow, moving towards the edge of a dense thicket of young spruce. "Just gonna take a quick look around. Stay put."

Quinn started to object, a knot of unease tightening in her stomach. "Marcus, wait. We should stick together."

But he was already moving, his figure disappearing behind the screen of dark green branches. They heard the faint crunch of his boots on the snow-covered ground, then silence.

A minute passed. Then two. The silence stretched, taut and unnatural. The only sound was the drip of melting snow from the branches above, a slow, steady rhythm like a ticking clock.

"Marcus?" Quinn called out, her voice low but urgent.

No response.

"Marcus!" Ben shouted, his voice cracking with renewed fear.

Still, only silence. A heavy, suffocating silence that seemed to press in on them from all sides.

Quinn exchanged a look with Sarah. The same unspoken fear was reflected in their eyes. She rose to her feet, her hand instinctively going to the canister of bear spray on her belt. "Stay here," she told Lila and Ben. "Sarah, come with me. Slowly. Quietly."

They moved towards the thicket where Marcus had disappeared, their hearts pounding a frantic rhythm against their ribs. The snow here was disturbed, Marcus's footprints clear and distinct. They followed them for a few yards, the dense branches of the young spruce trees pressing in on them, obscuring their vision.

"Marcus?" Quinn whispered, peering through the foliage.

And then, Sarah let out a small, stifled cry, her hand flying to her mouth. Quinn pushed past a low-hanging branch and saw what Sarah had seen.

It was a boot. Marcus's boot. A sturdy, insulated hiking boot, lying on its side in the snow, as if it had been casually kicked off.

But it wasn't empty.

Protruding from the top of the boot, stark and horrifying against the white snow, was the severed stump of an ankle, bone and gristle starkly visible. And still encased within the boot, presumably, was Marcus's foot, and at least one toe. The snow around the boot was stained a horrifying, brilliant red.

Quinns stomach heaved. She fought back a wave of nausea, her mind reeling from the sheer, brutal savagery of it. Marcus was gone. Vanished without a sound, without a struggle, leaving behind this gruesome, personal token. It was a message, as clear and terrifying as the animal totem. *We can take you whenever we want. We can leave pieces of you behind.*

Lila and Ben, drawn by Sarah's choked cry, had followed them. Lila saw the boot and let out a thin, keening wail, her camera falling from her numb fingers into the snow. Ben simply stared, his face a mask of utter, catatonic horror.

Quinn forced herself to think, to act. "We have to go," she said, her voice hoarse, grabbing Lila's arm. "Now. He's gone. There's nothing we can do for him." The words felt like ashes in her mouth. Marcus, the stoic, capable crewman, reduced to a bloody remnant in the snow.

Lila, surprisingly, seemed to rally. She picked up her camera, her movements jerky, her face streaked with tears. "I… I filmed," she stammered, her eyes wide and unfocused. "When he walked away. I was… I was still filming."

"Later," Quinn said, her voice firm. "We look at it later. We have to move. Now. Before it comes back for us."

They fled, a desperate, stumbling retreat, leaving the gruesome relic of Marcus behind in the red-stained snow. The forest, which had seemed merely oppressive, now felt actively malevolent, alive with unseen eyes, every shadow a potential hiding place for the thing that hunted them.

They ran until their lungs burned and their legs ached, until they could run no more. They found themselves on a steep, rocky slope, the trees thinning out slightly, offering a wider, if more exposed, view of the surrounding wilderness. Below them, the forest stretched out like a dark, undulating sea.

It was here, huddled behind a jagged outcrop of rock, that Lila finally played back the footage on her camera. Her hands shook so violently that Quinn had to steady the small device.

The footage was chaotic, filmed from a low angle as Lila had been sitting on the ground. It showed Marcus getting up, his back to the camera, then walking towards the spruce thicket. He disappeared from view. The camera remained focused on the empty space for a few seconds. Then, just as Lila was presumably about to stop recording, there was a flicker of movement in the background, deep within the shadows of the spruce trees.

"There!" Ben whispered, his finger jabbing at the small screen. "Freeze it! Freeze it there!"

Lila fumbled with the controls, her breath catching in her throat. She managed to pause the footage.

It was only a frame or two, blurred and indistinct, almost subliminal. But it was there. A shape, tall and dark, moving with impossible speed between the trees. It was not an animal. It was upright, with long, powerful limbs and a massive, hunched torso. Its head was indistinct, lost in shadow, but the overall impression was one of immense power and terrifying, unnatural grace. It was there, in the same frame as Marcus's retreating figure, and then, in the next frame, it was gone, as was Marcus.

A collective gasp escaped them. This was it. This was the thing that had derailed the train, the thing that had created the gruesome totem, the thing that had taken Hammond, and now Marcus.

Quinn stared at the frozen image, her blood running cold. She had spent years studying predators, their behavior, their territorial imperatives. What she was seeing here, what they were experiencing, was a terrifying perversion of natural law. This was an apex predator, yes, but one that operated with a level of cunning, cruelty, and ritualistic intelligence that defied any biological explanation. It was not just hunting them for food. It was toying with them, terrorizing them, sending them messages in blood and bone.

"It… it was right there," Sarah whispered, her voice filled with horrified awe. "He never stood a chance."

Lila stared at the image on her camera, her face pale. The implications of what she had captured, what she was now a witness to, seemed to weigh heavily on her. She tried to connect her camera to her phone, a desperate, futile gesture. "No signal," she muttered, her voice flat. "Of course, no signal. No one will ever see this. No one will ever believe this." The carefully constructed world of her online influence, her millions of followers, her brand partnerships – it all seemed like a distant, absurd dream in the face of this raw, visceral horror. Her control was gone. Her content was a scream in the void.

Quinn knew they couldn't stay there. They were exposed on the slope. But where could they go? The forest below was a hunting ground. The mountains above were treacherous and offered no guarantee of safety.

"We keep moving," Quinn said, her voice heavy with a weariness that went beyond physical exhaustion. "We try to find shelter before dark. Real shelter. A cave, an overhang, anything." She took the flare gun from her pack. Two flares left. Two chances to signal for a rescue that felt increasingly unlikely.

Meanwhile, back at the wreckage of The Borealis Express, the discovery of Hammond's grotesquely displayed body had plunged the remaining survivors into a new depth of terror and despair. The flimsy barricades they had erected around the carriage now seemed like a child's defense against a tidal wave. The forest, with its shifting branches and watchful silence, pressed in on them, a living, breathing entity of unimaginable malevolence.

Alistair Prichard, after his initial violent reaction to seeing Hammond, had collapsed. He sat slumped against the wall of the carriage, his face grey, his eyes vacant. The visionary billionaire, the man who had sought to conquer the wilderness with luxury and steel, was broken.

Eleanor Ainsworth, despite her own fear and the throbbing pain from her head wound, tried to maintain some semblance of leadership, though her voice trembled and her hands shook. "We have to… we have to stay together," she urged, her gaze darting nervously towards the dark treeline. "No one goes out alone. No one."

Bruno, the chef, his face a mask of grim fury, had dragged himself closer to the barricaded entrance, his meat cleaver resting on his lap. His injured leg was clearly causing him immense pain, but his eyes, dark and burning, never left the forest. He muttered to himself in Italian, a stream of curses and what sounded like prayers.

The influencers, Chad and Kendal, were beyond hysterics now. They huddled together in a corner of the carriage, their faces buried in their hands, emitting small, whimpering sounds. Tiffany, the third influencer, had fallen into a state of near catatonia, staring blankly at the opposite wall, her body trembling uncontrollably. The curated lives they had so meticulously crafted had been shattered, leaving behind only raw, primal fear.

The elderly man who had been suffering from hypothermia had passed away quietly in the early afternoon, his frail body finally succumbing to the relentless cold. His death, while tragic, was almost a footnote to the larger, more immediate horror that gripped them. They covered his body with a blanket, another grim testament to their failing struggle.

As the sun began its slow descent, painting the sky in hues of blood orange and bruised purple, the atmosphere in the besieged carriage grew thick with an almost unbearable tension. Every snap of a twig, every gust of wind that rattled the broken windows, sent fresh jolts of terror through the huddled survivors. They knew, with a certainty that transcended logic, that the night would bring fresh horrors. The entity was out there, watching, waiting. Hammond's displayed body was a promise.

Darkness fell, swift and absolute. They had a single, flickering lantern, its fuel dwindling, casting long, dancing shadows that writhed and twisted like malevolent spirits. The fire outside had died down to a bed of glowing embers, offering little light and even less warmth.

The sounds started subtly, just as they had the night before. A distant rustle in the undergrowth. A soft, almost inaudible footfall. Then, closer, the distinct snap of a dry branch.

Bruno gripped his cleaver, his knuckles white. Eleanor held the heavy iron poker Prichard had dropped, her breath catching in her throat. Even Prichard himself seemed to stir, a flicker of awareness returning to his vacant eyes.

Then came the scream.

It was Tiffany. She had been huddled against the far wall, seemingly lost in her catatonic state. Suddenly, she shot bolt upright, her eyes wide with a terror that was beyond human comprehension. She pointed a shaking finger towards one of the shattered windows, its jagged edges black against the faint moonlight.

"It's there!" she shrieked, her voice cracking. "Looking in! Oh God, it's looking in!"

Before anyone could react, before they could even see what she was pointing at, the flimsy barricade at the carriage entrance exploded inwards with a sound like a thunderclap. Splintered wood and twisted metal flew through the air. A huge, dark shape filled the opening, silhouetted against the faint glow of the dying embers outside.

It was impossibly tall, its shoulders broad and hunched, its limbs long and powerful. Its features were lost in shadow, but two points of light, like burning coals, glinted where its eyes should be. A low, guttural growl rumbled from its chest, a sound that vibrated through the very floorboards of the carriage.

Chaos erupted. Screams tore through the confined space. Bruno, with a roar of defiance, lunged forward, swinging his cleaver wildly. The cleaver connected with something solid, a sickening thud, but the creature barely flinched.

A massive, hairy arm, impossibly long and powerful, shot out. It seized Tiffany around the waist, lifting her from the ground as if she weighed nothing. Her scream was cut short as she was dragged, kicking and flailing, towards the shattered entrance.

"No!" Eleanor screamed, lunging forward with the poker, but she was too slow, too late.

Tiffany was pulled through the opening with horrifying speed, her last, choked cry swallowed by the darkness outside. There was a brief, terrible sound of a struggle, a muffled thud, then silence. A chilling, absolute silence.

The creature was gone. Tiffany was gone.

The remaining survivors stared at the gaping hole in their barricade, their faces frozen in masks of disbelief and utter terror. Bruno lay on the floor, groaning, clutching his arm where the creature had swatted him aside. The cleaver lay a few feet away, its blade stained with a dark, viscous fluid that was not human blood.

Alistair Prichard was babbling incoherently, his eyes rolling back in his head. Chad and Kendal were screaming, their voices raw and hoarse. Eleanor stood frozen, the iron poker hanging uselessly in her hand, her mind struggling to comprehend the swift, brutal violence she had just witnessed.

The red snow around their encampment, stained by Hammond's gruesome fate, now held the fresh promise of more. The entity was not just watching. It was actively culling them, one by one, with a terrifying efficiency and a chilling, almost contemptuous ease. The night was far from over.

Chapter 6 – False Shelter

The frozen image on Lila's camera—the shadowy, impossibly swift figure that had been Marcus's doom—burned itself into Quinn's retinas. It was a confirmation of their deepest, most primal fears, a visual testament to the malevolent force that stalked them. They were exposed on the rocky slope, the fading light painting the vast, indifferent wilderness in hues of bruised purple and blood orange. Night was coming, and with it, the full terror of the unseen.

"We have to move," Quinn repeated, her voice a hoarse whisper, shoving the horror down, forcing pragmatic thought to the surface. "Find cover. Anything. Before it's completely dark."

Ben was shaking uncontrollably, his face ashen. "Cover? Where? It's everywhere! It saw us, it knows where we are!"

"It knew where Marcus was too," Sarah said, her voice flat, devoid of inflection, her gaze fixed on the darkening forest below. "It didn't matter."

Lila, surprisingly, was the one who seemed to find a sliver of resolve in the face of utter despair. She switched off her camera, the small click loud in the sudden silence. "Quinn's right. Sitting here is death. Moving is... maybe death. But at least we're doing something." She looked at Quinn, her eyes, usually so adept at reflecting curated emotion, now held a raw, desperate plea for direction.

They stumbled onward, driven by the encroaching darkness and the chilling memory of Marcus's fate. Quinn pushed them upwards, away from the denser forest, hoping to find a cave, an overhang, any natural feature that might offer even a modicum of protection. The terrain was treacherous, a jumble of loose scree and sharp-edged boulders, their progress agonizingly slow. Every shadow seemed to writhe with unseen menace, every gust of wind carried imagined whispers.

The last vestiges of sunlight bled from the sky, leaving behind a cold, star-dusted blackness. The temperature plummeted, and the wind, unimpeded on the exposed slope, cut through their inadequate clothing like knives. Quinn knew hypothermia was now as much a threat as the creature that hunted them.

It was Ben, his teeth chattering audibly, who spotted it first. A dark shape, a little way down from their precarious path, nestled at the base of a sheer rock face, partially obscured by a thicket of skeletal, snow-dusted bushes. "What's… what's that?" he stammered, pointing with a trembling finger.

Quinn squinted into the gloom. It looked… structured. Too regular to be a natural rock formation. A faint, almost imperceptible hope flickered within her. "Stay here," she ordered, her voice low. She unclipped the heavy flashlight from her belt, its beam weak but better than nothing, and cautiously approached the shape.

As she drew closer, pushing aside the brittle branches, her heart leaped. It was a building. Or what was left of one. A small, dilapidated cabin, its log walls weathered and grey, its roof sagging precariously in places. A single, grimy window stared out like a blind eye. An abandoned ranger outpost, perhaps, or an old trapper's hut.

"Shelter," she breathed, the word a prayer. She waved the others forward.

Their relief was palpable, a brief, intoxicating wave that momentarily washed away their terror. A structure. Walls. A roof. It was a fragile shield against the vast, hostile wilderness, but it was something.

The door, made of rough-hewn planks, hung crookedly on one rusted hinge. Quinn pushed it inward with the toe of her boot. It creaked open with a groan that echoed in the stillness, revealing a dark, musty interior.

"Hello?" Quinn called out, her voice tentative, though she knew, with a chilling certainty, that no human would answer. The flashlight beam cut through the darkness, illuminating a single, small room. Dust lay thick on every surface, cobwebs draped like macabre decorations. A rough-hewn table and two rickety chairs stood in the center of the room. A rusty wood-burning stove occupied one corner, its stovepipe long since collapsed. In another corner, a crude bunk bed, its mattress rotted and spilling its stuffing, sagged against the wall.

The air was heavy with the smell of decay, disuse, and something else… a faint, lingering scent that made the hairs on the back of Quinn's neck prickle. It was a coppery, metallic tang, like old, dried blood.

"It's… it's something," Sarah said, her voice trembling slightly as she stepped inside, her eyes wide as she took in the squalor.

Lila followed, her earlier bravado fading as she absorbed the grim reality of their refuge. Ben huddled near the doorway, as if afraid to venture further into the oppressive gloom.

"We secure the door," Quinn said, trying to inject a note of confidence into her voice. "Ben, Sarah, see if you can find anything to wedge against it. Lila, keep an eye out the window. I'm going to check the rest of this place." Though 'rest of this place' was an overstatement. It was a single, claustrophobic room.

While Ben and Sarah managed to prop one of the rickety chairs against the door, creating a flimsy barricade, Quinn swept the flashlight beam around the cabin. Her eyes fell on the far wall, near the bunk bed. Scratched into the wooden logs, almost obscured by grime and shadows, were carvings.

Not random marks. Symbols. Some were crude representations of animals – a bear, a wolf, a raven. Others were more abstract, geometric patterns that seemed to hold a strange, unsettling significance. And among them, repeated several times, was a symbol that made her blood run cold: a tall, stick-like figure with elongated limbs and a horned head. The same figure she had seen etched into the cedar tree near the train wreckage.

"Quinn?" Lila whispered, her voice tight with fear. "What is it?"

Quinn directed the flashlight beam onto the carvings. A collective gasp went up from the small group.

"It's been here before," Sarah breathed, her hand covering her mouth. "Whatever it is… it's been here."

The initial relief of finding shelter had evaporated, replaced by a new, more insidious dread. This was not a refuge. This was a place that had known the entity, a place that bore its marks.

Quinn's attention was drawn to something else, tucked beneath the lower bunk, almost hidden in the shadows. A small, leather-bound book, its cover warped and stained. She picked it up, her fingers trembling slightly. It was a journal.

She opened it carefully, the pages brittle and yellowed with age. The ink was faded, the handwriting spidery and difficult to decipher in the dim flashlight beam.

"October 17th, 1978," she read aloud, her voice barely a whisper. *"The snows came early this year. Traplines are poor. Something is spooking the game. Heard strange calls in the night again. Not wolf, not bear. Something… other."*

She turned a page. *"November 3rd, 1978. Found tracks by the creek. Bigger than any bear. Made by no beast I know. Old Joseph down at the settlement warned me about this place. Said the K'eyghot'an call it 'The Land of Lost Souls.' Said something ancient guards these woods. Laughed at him then. Not laughing now."*

A chill snaked down Quinn's spine. She continued to read, her voice a low murmur, the others huddled around her, listening in horrified silence. The journal chronicled the descent of a solitary trapper, a man named Octavius Becker, into fear and madness. He wrote of dwindling supplies, of game vanishing, of strange, unsettling sounds in the night. He described finding ritualistic arrangements of bones and feathers, of feeling watched, hunted.

"December 1st, 1978. It came to the cabin last night. Didn't see it. Just heard it. Circling. Scratching at the door. The sounds it made… God forgive me, the sounds… It knows I'm here. It's toying with me."

The final entry was short, scrawled, almost illegible. *"December 5th, 1978. No escape. It's in the trees. It's in my head. The eyes… always the eyes… LEAVE THIS PLACE. LEAVE OR BECOME PART OF THE SILENCE…"*

The journal ended there. The remaining pages were blank.

A heavy silence filled the small cabin, broken only by Ben's ragged breathing. The words of Octavius Becker, written nearly half a century ago, echoed their own terrifying reality. They were not the first. This was an ancient horror, a recurring nightmare.

"He… he knew," Sarah whispered, her face pale. "He knew what was out here."

Lila, who had been filming Quinn reading the journal, slowly lowered her camera. Her face was a mask of stunned comprehension. "This whole time…" she murmured. "This whole place… it's a trap."

The flimsy security of their shelter felt like a cruel joke. They were in a place marked by the entity, a place where another soul had succumbed to its terror.

Quinn closed the journal, her mind racing. The warnings, the carvings, Octavius Becker's descent into madness – it all painted a horrifying picture. But there was no time for despair. Night had fallen completely. The wind howled outside, rattling the loose timbers of the cabin, sounding like the mournful cries of lost souls.

"We stay alert," Quinn said, her voice firmer than she felt. "Take turns watching. Two at the window, one at the door. Try to get some rest if you can. We'll need our strength if we're going to make it through the night."

The hours that followed were an eternity of taut nerves and suffocating fear. The flimsy barricade at the door seemed pitifully inadequate. The single grimy window offered a terrifyingly limited view of the black, snow-swept wilderness outside. Every creak of the old cabin, every gust of wind, every rustle in the surrounding bushes, sent fresh jolts of adrenaline through them.

Lila, surprisingly, volunteered for the first watch with Quinn. The shared horror seemed to have forged an unlikely bond between them. Ben and Sarah huddled together on the dusty floor, wrapped in the single shared blanket, their eyes wide and fearful.

Outside, the forest seemed alive with unseen movement. Shadows danced in the periphery of their vision. They heard sounds – the snap of a twig, a soft footfall, a low, guttural cough that was too deep, too resonant, to be human. Were they real, or products of their frayed nerves and overactive imaginations? It was impossible to tell.

Quinn clutched the flare gun, her finger resting on the trigger. Two flares left. Two chances. But what good would they be if the rescue they signaled for arrived too late, or found only what Octavius Becker had become: a part of the silence?

It was sometime after midnight, during Sarah's and Ben's watch, that the first direct assault came. Quinn and Lila had been trying to get some fitful, uneasy sleep on the rotted bunk, the trapper's journal clutched in Quinn's hand.

A sudden, violent crash from the direction of the door jolted them awake. Ben screamed, a high-pitched sound of pure terror. The chair they had wedged against the door splintered, flying across the room. The door itself shuddered, then burst inward with a sound like a gunshot, ripped from its single remaining hinge.

A massive, dark shape filled the doorway, silhouetted against the faint, snowy light from outside. It was taller than a man, broader than any bear, its outline a terrifying parody of the human form. Two eyes, like burning coals, fixed on them from the darkness of its unseen face. A low, guttural growl rumbled from its chest, a sound that vibrated through the very floorboards.

Sarah, who had been standing near the door, screamed and scrambled backwards, tripping over her own feet. Ben stood frozen, his mouth agape, his eyes wide with catatonic horror.

Quinn reacted on pure instinct. She lunged for the flare gun, her fingers fumbling with the cold metal. "Get back!" she yelled, aiming the gun towards the monstrous shape in the doorway.

The creature took a step into the cabin, its immense bulk seeming to suck all the air from the small space. A long, impossibly powerful arm, covered in coarse, dark hair, reached out towards Ben.

Quinn fired.

The flare erupted with a deafening roar and a blinding flash of crimson light, momentarily illuminating the cabin in a hellish, demonic glow. The creature recoiled, letting out a deafening, enraged shriek, a sound that was part animal, part something else entirely, something that clawed at their sanity. It raised an arm to shield its eyes from the sudden, intense light.

In that brief, terrifying illumination, Quinn saw it. Not clearly, not fully, but enough. Its face was a nightmarish landscape of matted fur, a flattened, snout-like nose, and a wide, lipless mouth filled with jagged, yellowed teeth. Its eyes, even in the glare of the flare, burned with a malevolent, ancient intelligence.

The flare arced past the creature, embedding itself in the snow outside, where it burned with a fierce, sputtering intensity, casting flickering, dancing shadows.

The creature, momentarily blinded and enraged, hesitated. It was enough.

"Out! Through the window!" Quinn screamed, grabbing Lila's arm and shoving her towards the single, grimy window on the opposite wall. "Go! Now!"

The window was small, its frame rotted. Sarah, recovering her senses, threw herself at it, smashing the remaining panes of glass with a piece of firewood she had grabbed. She scrambled through the opening, cutting herself on the jagged edges, but not stopping.

Lila followed, her movements clumsy with terror but driven by a desperate will to survive. Quinn pushed Ben towards the opening. He was still frozen, his eyes fixed on the creature, which was beginning to recover, its enraged growls growing louder.

"Ben, move!" Quinn yelled, shoving him hard. He stumbled, then seemed to snap out of his trance, scrambling towards the window.

The creature lunged. Quinn didn't wait. She turned and threw herself through the jagged opening, landing hard on the snow-covered ground outside, the impact jarring her already aching shoulder. She rolled, then scrambled to her feet, ignoring the searing pain from cuts on her arms and face.

Lila and Sarah were already running, stumbling through the deep snow, away from the cabin, towards the relative darkness of the trees. Ben was just ahead of Quinn, his breath coming in ragged, panicked gasps.

They didn't look back. They couldn't. The sounds from within the cabin – the enraged roars of the creature, the crash of furniture, the splintering of wood – were enough to fuel their desperate flight.

They ran blindly, with no sense of direction, their only thought to put as much distance as possible between themselves and the horror they had unleashed. The burning flare behind them cast long, monstrous shadows that seemed to chase them, to nip at their heels.

They had found shelter, yes. A false shelter. A place that had amplified their terror, a place that had brought them face to face with the ancient, malevolent entity that ruled these woods.

They had escaped, for now. But one of them had not.

As they stumbled through a dense thicket of young pines, gasping for breath, Quinn realized with a sickening lurch of her stomach that Ben was no longer with them. She looked back, her heart pounding. He wasn't there. He hadn't made it out of the cabin. Or if he had, he hadn't made it far.

A new sound cut through the night, from the direction of the ranger station. A single, high-pitched scream of utter agony, abruptly cut short. Then, a series of sickening, wet tearing sounds, followed by a low, guttural growl that sounded almost… satisfied.

Ben was gone.

Quinn, Lila, and Sarah huddled together in the freezing darkness, the sounds from the cabin echoing in their minds, Ben's final scream a fresh wound in their already shattered psyches. The false shelter had claimed another victim.

Lila, her face streaked with tears and grime, her camera clutched forgotten in her hand, finally broke. "No more," she whispered, her voice hoarse, her body shaking uncontrollably. "I can't… I can't film this. It's… it's too much. It's not content. It's just… horror." She let the camera fall from her grasp, its lens staring blankly up at the indifferent stars.

Quinn watched the camera fall. The last working GoPro, the one that held the only visual evidence of Marcus's demise, lay useless in the snow. With a surge of desperate pragmatism, she bent and retrieved it, pocketing the small device. If any of them made it out, the world had to know. Even if the world chose not to believe.

They were three now. Lost, freezing, hunted. And the night was still young.

As if to punctuate their despair, a new, chilling message became apparent as the first, faint light of dawn began to touch the eastern sky, revealing the snow-covered ground around the area where they had taken refuge after fleeing the cabin.

Spelled out in a horrifying, meticulous arrangement of dark pine needles, stark against the white snow, was a single, unequivocal word:

LEAVE.

The entity was not just hunting them. It was communicating. It was ordering them out of its domain. But leaving, Quinn knew, was not an escape. It was merely a slower, more terrifying path into the heart of its territory, into the depths of its ancient, malevolent power. The false shelter had been a lesson. The real test of survival was just beginning.

Chapter 7 – Cull

The word lay stark against the canvas of the dawn-lit snow: LEAVE. Etched in meticulously arranged pine needles, it was a pronouncement, a judgment delivered by the ancient, unseen warden of this frozen hell. Quinn stared at it, the single, brutal syllable a final, crushing blow to any lingering, desperate hope that they might have misunderstood, that they might have imagined the malevolent intelligence guiding the horrors of the past days. Ben's final, agonized scream, a phantom echo from the direction of the blood-soaked cabin, was still fresh in her ears.

Lila, her face a mask of tear-streaked grime and hollow-eyed shock, stood beside her, trembling uncontrollably. The bravado, the resilience she had shown earlier, had been shattered by the cabin attack and Ben's horrific end. Her expensive camera, now clutched by Quinn, felt like a dead weight, a useless artifact from a world that no longer existed.

Sarah, the architect, was a study in pale, silent terror. She hugged herself, her gaze darting nervously towards the oppressive wall of trees that encircled them, as if expecting the monstrous figure from the cabin to materialize at any moment.

"Leave…" Lila whispered, her voice a dry, rasping sound. "It wants us to leave. So we leave. We just… walk away. Anywhere."

Quinn shook her head, a cold, grim certainty settling within her. "No," she said, her voice low but firm. "It's not a suggestion. It's a command. And it's a trap." She gestured towards the vast, snow-choked wilderness that stretched in every direction, a labyrinth of silent, watchful trees and treacherous, hidden ravines. "Leave to where? Into its embrace? It's herding us. Toying with us. This entire forest is its killing ground."

The trapper Octavius Becker's final, desperate words from the journal echoed in her mind: *LEAVE OR BECOME PART OF THE SILENCE*. Leaving was not an escape; it was a surrender to a slower, more agonizing demise.

"Then what do we do?" Sarah asked, her voice barely audible, laced with a despair that mirrored Quinn's own. "We can't stay here. We can't go back to the cabin. And it seems we can't... leave."

Quinn's gaze swept their surroundings. They were exposed, exhausted, their meager supplies dwindling. The single remaining flare in her pocket felt like a cruel joke. Hypothermia was a gnawing threat, the biting wind relentless. But surrender was not an option. Not yet.

"The train," Quinn said, a desperate plan forming in her mind. "The others. If any of them are still alive... there's strength in numbers, however small. And the creature... it struck the cabin last night. It might believe it's finished with this area, with us. It might have returned its attention to the wreckage." It was a slim hope, a gamble based on the terrifying, unknowable calculus of the entity's motives, but it was better than wandering blindly into the wilderness to be picked off one by one.

"Go back there?" Lila recoiled, her eyes wide with remembered horror. "After what happened to Hammond? After Tiffany?"

"It's our only chance, Lila," Quinn insisted, her voice gentle but firm. "We know the general direction. If we can reach them, warn them further, maybe... maybe we can make a stand. Or at least die fighting together, not scattered and alone."

The thought of returning to the scene of such carnage, to the place where Hammond's mutilated body still hung as a gruesome sentinel, was terrifying. But the alternative, to obey the entity's command and walk into the deeper wilderness, felt like a quicker path to oblivion.

With a heavy, shared silence of grim acceptance, they began to move. Quinn led, trying to retrace their panicked flight from the previous night, using the rising sun as a crude compass. The GoPro camera, tucked into her pocket, was a cold, hard reminder of their lost companions, of the horrors they had witnessed. If she survived, the world would see. Even if it refused to believe.

The journey back towards the train line was a torturous ordeal. Their fear was a constant companion, every shadow a potential threat, every snap of a twig a jolt to their frayed nerves. They moved slowly, cautiously, acutely aware that they were intruders in a domain ruled by an ancient, implacable power.

Meanwhile, at the mangled wreckage of The Borealis Express, the dawn had brought no solace, only a clearer view of their desperate, besieged reality. The gaping hole in their barricade, torn open by the creature when it had snatched Tiffany, was a stark reminder of their vulnerability. Bruno, the chef, lay propped against a pile of cushions, his arm, where the creature had swatted him, a swollen, purplish mass. The pain was immense, but his dark eyes, burning with a mixture of agony and furious defiance, never left the treeline. He clutched his meat cleaver, its blade still bearing the dark, viscous fluid of the entity – a fluid that had begun to smoke faintly as the first rays of sunlight touched it, emitting a faint, acrid odor before drying to a black, resinous crust.

Eleanor Ainsworth, her face etched with exhaustion and grief, moved among the few remaining survivors like a ghost. Alistair Prichard, the billionaire, had retreated into a state of near catatonia, muttering incoherently, his eyes vacant. Chad and Kendal, the influencers, were huddled together, their earlier terror having subsided into a dull, whimpering apathy. They were broken shells, their carefully constructed online personas shattered by the raw, visceral horror of their reality.

"We can't stay here," Bruno rasped, his voice hoarse with pain. He gestured with his good hand towards the violated barricade. "It will come back. It knows we are weak. It is… *assaggiando*… tasting us. One by one."

Eleanor looked at him, her eyes filled with a despair that mirrored his own. "But where can we go, Bruno? Hammond… Tiffany… the forest is… it's death."

"Death is here too, *cara*," Bruno said, his gaze unwavering. "But if we move, perhaps we find a different death. A quicker one. Or perhaps… perhaps a chance." He tried to push himself up, a groan of agony escaping his lips. "The river. Hammond spoke of a river, not far from the line. If we can reach it, follow it downstream… it might lead somewhere. Anywhere but here."

The thought of venturing out into the open, of leaving the flimsy, blood-soaked sanctuary of the wrecked carriage, was terrifying. But Bruno was right. Staying meant waiting for the creature to return, to pick them off at its leisure. Moving offered a sliver of hope, however faint, however desperate.

Eleanor nodded slowly, a flicker of resolve returning to her weary eyes. "Alright, Bruno. The river." She looked at the others. "We have to try."

Their preparations were hasty, desperate. They had little to take – a few tattered blankets, the last of their water, the heavy iron poker Eleanor still carried. Alistair Prichard had to be helped to his feet, his movements stiff and uncoordinated, his eyes still lost in some private hell. Chad and Kendal followed numbly, like sheep being led to the slaughter.

Bruno, despite his grievous injury, insisted on taking the lead, his meat cleaver held ready. He moved with a painful, dragging gait, but his spirit, fueled by a potent cocktail of rage and a primal will to survive, was unbroken.

They stumbled out of the wrecked carriage, into the cold, grey light of mid-morning, a pathetic, broken procession. The forest watched them, silent and menacing. Hammond's body still hung from the spruce tree, a grotesque, swaying sentinel, a constant reminder of the fate that awaited them.

It was as they were passing this grim monument that the entity chose to strike again.

There was no warning, no sound, just a sudden, blurring movement from the dense thicket of trees beside the railway line. A massive, dark shape erupted from the shadows, moving with a speed that defied its immense bulk.

"*Attenzione!*" Bruno roared, spinning with surprising agility for an injured man, his cleaver raised.

The creature was on him in an instant. It was the same monstrous figure from the cabin, its eyes burning with a cold, malevolent fire, its lipless mouth drawn back in a silent snarl, revealing rows of jagged, yellowed teeth.

Bruno met its charge with a bellow of pure, untamed fury. He swung the cleaver with all his might, aiming for the creature's head. The heavy blade connected with a sickening thud, striking the side of the entity's skull. Dark, viscous fluid, the same that had coated the cleaver before, sprayed into the air.

The creature staggered back, a guttural roar of pain and rage tearing from its throat. For a fleeting second, it seemed stunned. But only for a second.

With a speed that was terrifying to behold, it recovered, its massive, clawed hand lashing out. It caught Bruno across the chest, the impact sending him flying backwards, his cleaver clattering onto the snow-covered ground.

Bruno landed hard, a pained cry ripped from his lips. He tried to scramble up, to reach for his weapon, but the creature was too fast. It loomed over him, its shadow falling like a shroud.

"No!" Eleanor screamed, lunging forward with the iron poker, but Alistair Prichard, in a moment of unexpected, panicked strength, grabbed her arm, pulling her back.

"Don't!" he shrieked, his eyes wide with terror. "It'll take you too!"

The creature's massive hand descended. It seized Bruno by the throat, lifting him effortlessly from the ground. Bruno's legs kicked feebly, his hands clawing at the crushing grip. His eyes, wide and bulging, fixed on Eleanor, a silent, desperate plea.

Then, his scream, a sound of unimaginable agony and defiance, cut off abruptly, mid-word, as a sickening, wet crunching sound echoed through the frozen air.

The creature held Bruno's limp body aloft for a moment, a horrifying trophy, then, with a contemptuous flick of its wrist, tossed him aside like a broken doll. Bruno's body landed in a crumpled heap in the snow, his neck twisted at an unnatural angle, his dark eyes staring sightlessly at the indifferent sky.

The chef, the brave, defiant Bruno, was dead.

The remaining survivors – Eleanor, Alistair, Chad, and Kendal – stood frozen, their minds reeling from the swift, brutal violence they had just witnessed. The creature turned its burning gaze upon them, a low, guttural growl rumbling in its chest. It took a step towards them.

Panic, raw and overwhelming, finally shattered their paralysis. They turned and fled, stumbling blindly along the railway line, away from the horror, away from Bruno's lifeless body, their screams swallowed by the vast, uncaring wilderness.

The creature did not pursue immediately. It watched them go, its head tilted slightly, as if contemplating its next move. Then, with a slow, deliberate movement, it bent and picked up Bruno's fallen meat cleaver, examining the heavy blade with a chilling, almost curious detachment before vanishing back into the silent, watchful trees.

Quinn, Lila, and Sarah, drawn by the faint, abruptly silenced scream that had carried on the wind, arrived at the edge of the clearing near the train wreckage minutes later. They saw Bruno's body lying in the snow, the scene of horrific, fresh violence. They saw the tracks of the other survivors, leading away along the railway line. And they saw the massive, unmistakable prints of the entity, heading in the same direction.

"They're alive," Quinn breathed, a mixture of relief and renewed dread churning within her. "Some of them. It's after them."

There was no time for grief, no time for hesitation. They followed the tracks, their own exhaustion forgotten in the desperate urgency of the moment. The path led them away from the railway line, down a steep, snow-covered embankment towards the sound of rushing water – a frozen riverbed, its surface a treacherous expanse of slick ice and snow-covered boulders.

They found the others, or what was left of them, at the edge of a narrow, ice-choked gorge through which the river flowed. Eleanor and Alistair were there, huddled together, their faces masks of terror. Chad lay a short distance away, his body contorted, his eyes wide with a silent scream, a dark stain spreading on the snow beneath him. He was clearly dead, his chest caved in as if by some unimaginable force.

Of Kendal, there was no sign.

"It ambushed us," Eleanor sobbed, her voice hoarse, as Quinn and the others reached them. "It came from the trees… so fast… Chad… he didn't stand a chance." She pointed a trembling finger towards the gorge. "Kendal… it dragged her… dragged her towards that crevasse."

Quinn looked towards the dark, narrow fissure in the rock face, a black wound in the side of the gorge. A few scattered items of clothing – a brightly colored scarf, a single glove – lay on the snow near its edge, a pathetic trail leading to the abyss. Kendal was gone, swallowed by the darkness, another victim of the entity's relentless cull.

Alistair Prichard was babbling, his eyes darting wildly. "The eyes… the burning eyes… it's not a beast… it's a devil… a devil from the ice…"

Suddenly, a shower of rocks and snow cascaded down from the top of the gorge wall above them. They looked up, their hearts leaping into their throats.

Silhouetted against the pale grey sky, standing on the precipice, was the creature. It was looking down at them, its massive form radiating an aura of pure, predatory menace. In one hand, it held Bruno's meat cleaver, the polished steel glinting faintly in the weak sunlight.

It let out a deafening roar, a sound that echoed off the canyon walls, a triumphant, terrifying declaration of its absolute dominion.

Then, it began to descend. Not climbing, but leaping from ledge to ledge with an impossible, terrifying agility, dislodging rocks and snow as it came, its burning eyes fixed on the small, terrified group huddled below.

"Run!" Quinn screamed, grabbing Lila's arm. "Move! Towards the river!"

They scrambled onto the frozen riverbed, their boots slipping on the slick ice. Sarah was just ahead of them, her breath coming in ragged gasps. Eleanor and Alistair stumbled behind, their movements clumsy with terror.

The creature landed on the riverbed with a ground-shaking thud, cutting off their retreat. It was between them and the direction they had come from, blocking any escape back up the embankment.

They were trapped.

Sarah, in her panic, veered too close to the edge of the frozen river, where the ice was thin. With a sickening crack, the ice gave way beneath her. She cried out, her arms flailing, as she plunged into the frigering, dark water below.

"Sarah!" Quinn screamed, lunging towards the hole, but Lila pulled her back.

"No, Quinn! You can't! It's too late!"

Sarah's head surfaced once, her eyes wide with terror and the shock of the icy water. She reached out a desperate hand, then, with a choked gasp, was pulled under by the strong current, disappearing beneath the churning, ice-choked water. She did not resurface.

Quinn stared at the dark, swirling hole in the ice, her mind numb with horror. Sarah, the quiet, resilient architect, was gone. Another life extinguished, another friend lost.

The creature was advancing on them, its movements slow, deliberate, savoring their terror. Alistair Prichard, his mind finally snapping, let out a high-pitched shriek and charged directly at the monster, waving his arms madly. The creature swatted him aside with a contemptuous backhand, sending him sprawling onto the ice, where he lay still.

Eleanor, seeing Prichard fall, seemed to find a last, desperate reserve of courage. She raised the iron poker, her face a mask of defiance. "Get away from us, you monster!" she screamed.

The creature paused, its burning eyes fixing on her. It tilted its head, as if considering her futile gesture. Then, with a swift, brutal movement, it lunged.

Quinn didn't see what happened next. She grabbed Lila's hand, pulling her along the treacherous, ice-covered riverbed, away from the horror, away from Eleanor's final, defiant scream, which was abruptly cut short.

They ran, stumbling, falling, their lungs burning, their hearts pounding. They did not look back. They could not. The sounds behind them — the sickening thuds, the guttural growls, the wet, tearing noises — were too horrific to comprehend.

They ran until they could run no more, until they collapsed onto a snow-covered bank at a bend in the river, miles from the gorge, miles from the carnage.

They were alone. Utterly, terrifyingly alone.

Quinn looked at Lila, her own face streaked with tears, her body trembling with exhaustion and a grief so profound it threatened to consume her. Sarah was gone. Ben was gone. Marcus was gone. Bruno, Hammond, Tiffany, Chad, Kendal, Alistair, Eleanor… all gone. Victims of the cull.

They were the only ones left. The last two survivors of The Borealis Express.

Lila stared back at Quinn, her eyes hollow, reflecting the vast, empty sky. The transformation was complete. The image-obsessed influencer was dead, replaced by a hardened, traumatized witness, a survivor forged in the crucible of unimaginable horror.

"What… what do we do now?" Lila whispered, her voice barely audible above the mournful sigh of the wind.

Quinn looked around at the desolate, snow-covered landscape. The entity was still out there. It had culled the herd, but its hunt was not over. They were marked.

But they were still alive.

A spark of defiance, as fierce and unexpected as Bruno's last stand, ignited within Quinn. They would not become part of the silence. Not yet.

"We go back," Quinn said, her voice hoarse but resolute. She thought of the trapper's journal, of the cabin, of the single remaining flare. "We go back to the ranger station. It's the only place we know. We make a stand. Or we find a way to tell the world what happened here. We make them believe."

It was a desperate, almost suicidal plan. But it was a plan. And in the face of such overwhelming, malevolent power, a plan, however slim, was all they had left. The cull was over. The final, desperate struggle for survival had just begun.

Chapter 8 – Backtrack

The silence that descended after Quinn's desperate pronouncement – "We go back to the ranger station" – was heavy, thick with the ghosts of their fallen companions and the chilling certainty of their isolation. Lila stared at her, her eyes, once bright with the artificial sparkle of curated joy, now vast, dark pools reflecting a horror too profound for tears. The wind, a mournful, keening presence, whipped strands of matted hair across her grime-streaked face. They were the last. Two solitary figures in an immense, indifferent wilderness that had become a hunting ground, a charnel house.

"Back?" Lila's voice was a dry, rasping whisper, barely audible above the sigh of the wind through the skeletal, snow-laden trees. "To that... that place? Where Ben...?" She couldn't finish the sentence. The memory of the creature bursting into the cabin, of Ben's final, truncated scream, was a fresh, bleeding wound.

Quinn nodded, her own heart a leaden weight in her chest. Every instinct screamed at her to flee, to run until her lungs burned and her legs gave out, to put as much distance as possible between them and the horrors they had witnessed. But logic, cold and brutal, dictated otherwise. "It's the only structure we know for miles, Lila. The only place that offers even a sliver of a chance. The trapper's journal... he survived there for weeks, months even, before..." Before he became part of the silence. Quinn didn't voice the end of that thought. "And the flare.

Our last flare. If we're going to use it, it has to be from a place where it might be seen, where we can defend ourselves, even for a short while."

Defend themselves. Against a creature that had torn through metal, that had slaughtered trained men and terrified billionaires with contemptuous ease. It sounded like madness. Perhaps it was. But the alternative, to wander aimlessly, waiting for the inevitable, was a surrender Quinn was not yet ready to make.

Lila hugged herself, her body trembling not just from the biting cold but from the deep, bone-shaking trauma that had become her constant companion. "It knows that place, Quinn. It marked it. It... it wrote us a message there." The image of the word LEAVE, spelled out in meticulous pine needles, was seared into her memory.

"And it expects us to obey," Quinn said, her gaze sweeping the desolate landscape. "It expects us to run deeper into its territory. We do the unexpected. We go back. We fight. Or we die trying, on our own terms, not as... as sport."

A flicker of something – defiance, perhaps, or just the last vestiges of a desperate will to survive – sparked in Lila's hollow eyes. She straightened slightly, pulling her tattered, inadequate jacket tighter around herself. "Okay," she said, her voice still weak but with a new, ragged edge of resolve. "Okay, Quinn. Back to the cabin from hell."

The decision made, a grim, unspoken pact sealed between them, they began the arduous journey. Retracing their steps was a descent into a gallery of fresh horrors, each familiar landmark a monument to their lost friends, a testament to the entity's brutal, systematic cull.

The first trial was the river gorge. They approached it with trepidation, the roar of the unseen water beneath the ice a constant, menacing reminder of Sarah's fate. The dark, swirling hole where she had plunged into the frigid depths was still visible, a gaping wound in the frozen riverbed. Quinn averted her gaze, a fresh wave of grief washing over her. Sarah, the quiet, capable architect, swallowed by the icy darkness.

They found Alistair Prichard's body sprawled on the ice where the creature had swatted him aside. His eyes were wide, frozen in a rictus of terror, his expensive suit stiff with frost. Eleanor's iron poker lay a few feet away, a pathetic, useless weapon against such overwhelming power. Of Eleanor herself, there was no sign, only a wide, dark stain on the snow near the edge of the crevasse where Kendal had been dragged, a stain that spoke of a swift, brutal end.

Lila choked back a sob, turning away from the gruesome scene. Quinn paused only long enough to retrieve the iron poker. It was heavy, cold, but it was something. Another weapon, however inadequate, in their pitiful arsenal.

They climbed the embankment, away from the river of death, their movements slow, agonizing. The silence of the forest pressed in on them, broken only by their own ragged breathing and the crunch of their boots on the frozen snow. Every shadow seemed to hold a lurking menace, every rustle of leaves a prelude to attack.

Next came the site where Bruno had made his last, defiant stand. His body lay where the creature had tossed it, a crumpled, broken heap. The snow around him was churned and stained, a testament to the ferocity of his final moments. His meat cleaver was gone, taken by the entity, a chilling indication of its evolving, terrifying intelligence. It was not just a mindless beast; it was learning, adapting, arming itself.

Quinn knelt beside Bruno, her heart aching. The brave, passionate chef, who had faced death with such untamed fury. She gently closed his staring eyes, a small, inadequate gesture of respect. "Rest, Bruno," she whispered. "You fought well."

Lila stood a short distance away, her face pale, her arms wrapped tightly around herself. She couldn't look. The cumulative horror was too much, threatening to overwhelm her fragile composure.

As they were about to move on, Quinn's eye caught something half-buried in the snow near where Chad's body had lain – a small, dark object. She brushed away the snow. It was a smartphone, its screen cracked, but otherwise intact. Chad's phone.

A desperate, irrational hope flickered within her. A signal? A message? She pressed the power button. The screen remained stubbornly dark. The battery was dead. Useless. Another dead end.

She was about to toss it aside when she noticed a small, blinking red light near the camera lens. It was still recording. Or had been, until the battery died. Perhaps there was something on it. She pocketed the phone, another grim artifact for Lila's GoPro.

The journey continued, a relentless, soul-crushing trek through a landscape of death and despair. They passed the area where Marcus's boot, with its gruesome contents, had been found. The boot was gone now, the red snow a fading, brownish stain. The entity had reclaimed its grisly trophy.

The psychological toll of this backtracking was immense. Each step was a reminder of their losses, of their terrifying vulnerability. The forest seemed to watch them, its silence no longer indifferent but filled with a palpable, predatory intent. Quinn found herself constantly scanning the treeline, her hand never far from the canister of bear spray, her senses stretched to their breaking point.

Lila walked beside her like a phantom, her face a mask of numb shock. The transformation from the vibrant, self-obsessed influencer to this hollow-eyed survivor was complete and devastating. Yet, beneath the trauma, Quinn sensed a core of resilience, a stubborn refusal to completely surrender. She had seen too much, lost too much, to simply lie down and die.

It was late afternoon, the sky already beginning to bruise with the approach of another long, terrifying night, when the snow began to fall. At first, it was light, a gentle dusting of white flakes that seemed almost peaceful. But within minutes, the snowfall intensified, the flakes growing larger, heavier, driven by a rising wind. A snowstorm.

"No," Lila breathed, her voice filled with a new despair. "Not now."

The storm descended upon them with frightening speed, a white curtain dropping over the world, obscuring their vision, muffling sound, transforming the already hostile landscape into a disorienting, treacherous labyrinth. Visibility dropped to a few feet. The wind howled, a banshee wail that seemed to mock their plight, driving the snow into their faces, stinging their eyes, chilling them to the bone.

Navigation became almost impossible. Quinn tried to maintain her sense of direction, but the swirling snow and the featureless landscape offered few landmarks. They stumbled onward, buffeted by the wind, their tracks erased almost as soon as they were made. The forest, which had been a source of terror, now offered a perverse kind of shelter, the dense trees providing some minimal protection from the full fury of the storm, but also creating a claustrophobic, disorienting environment where danger could lurk unseen, inches away.

The sense of being hunted intensified with the storm. The swirling snow played tricks on their eyes, creating fleeting, monstrous shapes in the periphery of their vision. Every gust of wind sounded like a guttural growl, every falling branch like a stealthy footfall. The entity was out there, they knew it, perhaps using the storm as cover, stalking them, waiting for the opportune moment to strike.

They were cold, wet, and utterly exhausted. Hypothermia was no longer a distant threat; it was a gnawing, insidious reality. Quinn's fingers were numb, her movements clumsy.

Lila was shivering uncontrollably, her teeth chattering, her face a pale, bluish tinge.

"We have to… find shelter," Quinn yelled over the roar of the wind, her voice hoarse. "Keep moving. Don't stop." Stopping meant succumbing to the cold, to the despair, to the inevitable.

They blundered onward, two small, insignificant figures against the overwhelming power of the storm and the ancient, malevolent entity that ruled this frozen hell. Hope had dwindled to a tiny, flickering ember, threatening to be extinguished by the relentless onslaught of wind and snow.

It was in the deepest gloom of the storm, when they were at their most vulnerable, their senses dulled by cold and exhaustion, that the creature attacked.

There was no warning, no sound other than the howl of the wind. One moment, Lila was stumbling beside Quinn, her head bowed against the driving snow; the next, she was gone, snatched from Quinn's side with terrifying speed and silence.

Quinn spun around, her heart leaping into her throat. "Lila!" she screamed, her voice swallowed by the storm.

Through the swirling snow, she saw it – a massive, dark silhouette, impossibly tall, holding Lila's struggling form in one of its powerful arms. Lila was kicking and screaming, her cries thin and desperate against the roar of the wind, but her struggles were futile against the creature's immense strength. It was dragging her away, into the deeper shadows of the trees, towards a dark, narrow ravine Quinn hadn't noticed in the disorienting whiteness.

Quinn didn't think. She reacted. Pure, primal instinct, fueled by a desperate, protective rage, overwhelmed her fear and exhaustion. She lunged forward, the iron poker Eleanor had carried held high, a pathetic weapon against such a monstrous foe, but the only one she had.

"Let her go!" Quinn shrieked, charging into the swirling snow, towards the terrifying silhouette.

The creature paused, its head turning towards Quinn, its burning eyes, like coals in the storm-dimmed light, fixing on her. It let out a low, guttural growl, a sound that seemed to vibrate through the very air around them. It still held Lila pinned against its massive chest, her struggles growing weaker.

Quinn didn't hesitate. She swung the iron poker with all her might, aiming for the creature's head. The poker connected with a sickening thud, striking the side of its skull, the same spot Bruno had hit with his cleaver.

The creature roared, a sound of pure, unadulterated fury, staggering back a step. It loosened its grip on Lila momentarily, and Lila, seizing the opportunity, twisted free, falling to the snow-covered ground, gasping for breath.

But the creature recovered with terrifying speed. Its massive, clawed hand lashed out, not at Quinn, but at Lila, who was trying to scramble away. The claws, long and razor-sharp, raked across Lila's leg, tearing through her trousers and flesh, leaving deep, bleeding gashes.

Lila screamed, a sound of pure agony, collapsing onto the snow, clutching her mangled leg.

The creature loomed over her, its lipless mouth drawn back in a silent snarl, ready to deliver the killing blow.

Quinn knew she had only seconds. She dropped the poker, her numb fingers fumbling for the canister of bear spray on her belt. She ripped off the safety tab, her heart pounding a frantic rhythm against her ribs.

"Hey, ugly!" she screamed, her voice raw with desperation and defiance.

The creature turned its burning gaze towards her, momentarily distracted from its prey.

Quinn aimed and fired.

A dense, orange cloud of concentrated capsaicin erupted from the canister, engulfing the creature's head and upper body.

The effect was instantaneous and horrific. The creature shrieked, a sound of unimaginable pain and rage, a sound that tore through the storm, clawing at Quinn's sanity. It staggered back, its massive hands flying to its face, trying to wipe away the burning spray. It thrashed wildly, its roars echoing through the forest, dislodging snow from the overburdened branches.

Quinn didn't wait to see more. She scrambled to Lila's side, grabbing her arm. "Come on, Lila! We have to move! Now!"

Lila was sobbing, her face contorted in agony, but she tried to push herself up, her injured leg useless beneath her. "I can't… Quinn… I can't walk…"

"You have to!" Quinn insisted, pulling Lila to her feet, supporting her weight. "Lean on me! We have to get out of here before it recovers!"

They stumbled away, half-running, half-dragging, Lila leaning heavily on Quinn, leaving a trail of blood in the snow. Behind them, the creature's enraged, pain-filled roars continued, a terrifying soundtrack to their desperate flight. The bear spray had bought them a few precious moments, but Quinn knew it wouldn't hold the entity for long.

They blundered through the storm, driven by a primal fear and the fading sounds of the creature's fury. Quinn had no idea where they were going, her only thought to put as much distance as possible between them and the enraged monster. Lila was fading, her breath coming in shallow gasps, the blood from her leg staining the snow a horrifying crimson.

Just when Quinn thought they could go no further, when her own strength was failing, when the darkness of despair threatened to overwhelm her, she saw it. Through a momentary lull in the swirling snow, a dark, familiar shape loomed ahead – the sagging roofline, the blind eye of the single window.

The ranger station. The cabin from hell. Their last, desperate refuge.

With a final, superhuman effort, Quinn dragged Lila towards it, her own body screaming in protest. They reached the broken doorway, the scene of their earlier terrifying encounter. The interior was dark, cold, and filled with the ghosts of their lost companions.

Quinn helped Lila inside, collapsing with her onto the dusty, blood-stained floor. They were alive. Battered, bleeding, but alive. For now.

The storm raged outside, the wind howling like a hungry wolf. And somewhere out there, in the swirling whiteness, the creature, enraged and in pain, was recovering. It knew where they were. It would come for them.

Quinn looked at Lila, her friend's face pale and drawn, her eyes fluttering closed. She had to stop the bleeding. She had to keep Lila alive.

And then, she had to prepare for the final siege.

She fumbled in her pocket for the GoPro, its small, cold form a fragile link to the world they had lost. Then her fingers brushed against the last flare. One flare. One last chance.

But first… a signal. Octavius Becker's journal… Had he written anything about a radio? An emergency beacon? She vaguely recalled a passage, a desperate scrawl about his last attempts to contact the outside world, something about a transmitter… a repetitive pulse… a ping? She scanned the squalid cabin, her eyes searching for anything, any hope, in the deepening gloom. The trapper had been here for months. Surely, he would have had some way to call for help.

Her gaze fell upon a small, metal box tucked away in the darkest corner, beneath the rotted bunk, almost hidden by debris. It was old, rusted, but unmistakably an emergency locator beacon. Hope, fragile and unexpected, flickered anew. If she could get it to work…

The cull was over. The final stand was about to begin. And the trackless, remembering land waited, its silence pregnant with the promise of more blood in the snow.

Chapter 9 – Extraction

The wind howled a symphony of desolation around the flimsy walls of the ranger station, each gust threatening to tear the rotten timbers apart. Snow, driven with relentless fury, plastered itself against the grimy windowpane, a suffocating white shroud that mirrored the icy grip of despair tightening around Quinn's heart. Inside the squalid cabin, the air was frigid, thick with the metallic scent of Lila's blood and the lingering, musty odor of decay and old fear.

Lila lay on the dusty floor where Quinn had dragged her, her breath shallow, her face a ghastly, bluish white in the dim, flickering light of the single salvaged flashlight Quinn had propped against a wall. The deep gashes on her leg, inflicted by the creature's raking claws, oozed dark blood, staining her torn trousers and the grimy floorboards a horrifying crimson. She was shivering violently, her eyes fluttering, occasionally letting out small, whimpering moans of pain that tore at Quinn's already frayed nerves.

"Stay with me, Lila," Quinn murmured, her own voice hoarse, her fingers numb as she fumbled with the remnants of a tattered blanket she'd found in the cabin, trying to cover her friend, to offer some pitiful defense against the encroaching hypothermia. "You have to stay with me."

Her first priority was Lila's leg. Using strips of cloth torn from the rotting mattress ticking of the trapper's bunk – a grim echo of their first desperate attempts at first aid back at the train wreckage – Quinn tried to bind the wounds, to staunch the bleeding. Her hands were clumsy with cold and exhaustion, the makeshift bandages inadequate, but she worked with a desperate, focused intensity. Lila cried out, a thin, reedy sound, as Quinn tightened the bindings, the pain momentarily cutting through her shock.

"I know, I know it hurts," Quinn whispered, her own tears threatening to freeze on her lashes. "But we have to stop the bleeding. Just hold on."

Outside, the storm raged, a physical manifestation of the chaos and terror that had consumed their world. And somewhere in that swirling, white maelstrom, the creature, enraged by the bear spray, its hunt momentarily thwarted, was recovering. It knew they were here. This cabin, their last desperate refuge, was a trap, and the bait was their own fading lives.

Once Lila's wounds were as tended as Quinn could manage, her shivering somewhat lessened under the thin blanket, Quinn turned her attention to their only sliver of hope: the emergency locator beacon. The small, rusted metal box she had found tucked beneath the bunk felt impossibly heavy in her trembling hands. It was an ancient model, its casing dented, its labels faded and peeling. Would it even work? Had its batteries died decades ago, along with Octavius Becker's hope?

With fumbling fingers, she searched for a switch, a button, anything. The metal was cold, biting into her skin. She found a small, hinged panel on the side. It was rusted shut. Using the tip of the iron poker she had retrieved from the river gorge, she pried at it, her breath catching in her throat. The metal groaned in protest, then, with a sharp crack, the panel sprang open, revealing a small, corroded compartment.

Inside, nestled amongst crumbling insulation, were two cylindrical batteries, their casings green with verdigris. Quinn's heart sank. They looked ancient, hopelessly decayed. But there was also a small, red toggle switch, its plastic faded but intact, and a tiny, glass-covered light.

"Please," Quinn whispered, the word a desperate prayer to any god that might be listening in this forsaken corner of the world. "Please work."

She took a deep breath, her gaze flicking nervously towards the broken doorway, half-expecting the monstrous silhouette of the creature to appear at any moment. Then, with a trembling finger, she flipped the red toggle switch.

Nothing.

The tiny light remained dark. No reassuring beep, no flicker of life. Just cold, dead silence, punctuated by the howl of the wind and Lila's shallow, ragged breathing.

Despair, cold and absolute, threatened to engulf Quinn. This was it. Their last chance, extinguished before it even had a chance to ignite. They were truly alone, trapped, waiting for the inevitable.

But then, as she was about to toss the useless beacon aside, a faint, almost imperceptible crackle came from within the device. The tiny light flickered once, twice, then, miraculously, glowed a weak, hesitant green. A slow, rhythmic beep, barely audible above the storm, began to emanate from the rusted casing.

It was working.

Tears, hot and stinging, welled in Quinn's eyes, blurring her vision. Relief, so potent it was almost painful, washed over her, momentarily banishing the cold, the fear, the exhaustion. The beacon was active. A signal, however faint, however ancient, was pulsing outwards, a desperate cry for help from the heart of this frozen hell.

"Lila," Quinn choked out, her voice thick with emotion, crawling back to her friend's side. "Lila, it's working. The beacon… it's working."

Lila's eyes fluttered open, a flicker of comprehension in their hazy depths. A faint, ghost of a smile touched her lips. "Hope…" she whispered, her voice barely a breath.

But their reprieve, if it could even be called that, was short-lived. As if summoned by the beacon's desperate pulse, a new sound joined the chorus of the storm – a low, guttural growl, closer this time, just outside the cabin walls.

The creature was back.

Quinn's blood ran cold. She scrambled to her feet, grabbing the iron poker, her eyes darting towards the broken doorway. The flickering flashlight cast long, dancing shadows, transforming the familiar squalor of the cabin into a landscape of terror. The beacon continued its slow, rhythmic beep, a fragile heartbeat in the face of overwhelming menace.

"It's here," Lila whispered, her eyes wide with renewed fear.

Quinn positioned herself between Lila and the doorway, her knuckles white as she gripped the poker. Her body ached, her mind screamed for rest, but a surge of adrenaline, a primal instinct to protect, to survive, coursed through her veins. This was it. The final siege.

The scratching started then, a dry, rasping sound against the exterior wall of the cabin, near the grimy window. Long, deliberate scrapes, as if the creature were testing the rotten timbers, searching for a weakness. Quinn's heart hammered against her ribs. She could almost feel its presence, its malevolent intelligence, just inches away, separated only by a thin, decaying barrier of wood.

The scratching stopped. Silence, save for the howl of the wind and the steady beep of the beacon. Quinn held her breath, straining her ears, every nerve ending screaming.

Then, a thunderous crash from the roof. Wood splintered, dust and debris rained down. The creature was on top of the cabin, its immense weight making the entire structure groan and tremble. Quinn looked up, her eyes wide with horror, half-expecting the sagging roof to collapse, to bring the monster crashing down upon them.

More scraping, more tearing sounds, as the creature clawed at the roof timbers, trying to rip its way in. Lila let out a small, terrified whimper, burying her face in the tattered blanket.

Quinn knew they couldn't just wait. The cabin wouldn't hold. She had one flare left. One last, desperate gamble.

"Lila," she said, her voice tight, trying to keep the tremor out of it. "I'm going to use the flare. If anyone sees it… if the beacon is working… this might be our only chance to guide them."

She fumbled in her pocket for the flare gun, its cold, metallic form a small, inadequate comfort. She checked the cartridge, her fingers clumsy with cold and fear. One shot.

The creature's efforts on the roof intensified. A large piece of timber, rotten and splintered, crashed to the floor near Quinn's feet. The hole above them widened, revealing a patch of swirling, snow-filled sky, and then, for a horrifying instant, a monstrous, shadowy face, its eyes burning down at them with a cold, predatory fury.

Quinn didn't hesitate. She raised the flare gun, aiming it through the widening hole in the roof, towards the sky, towards any hope of salvation. She squeezed the trigger.

With a deafening roar and a blinding flash of crimson light, the flare shot upwards, a fiery serpent disappearing into the raging storm. For a moment, the interior of the cabin was bathed in an unearthly red glow, illuminating the terror on Lila's face, the desperation in Quinn's own eyes.

The creature on the roof shrieked, a sound of rage and perhaps surprise, recoiling from the sudden blast of light and heat. It scrambled back, its immense weight shaking the fragile structure.

The flare, Quinn prayed, would be visible above the storm, a beacon of distress in this desolate wilderness. But would anyone see it? And if they did, could they reach them in time?

The creature, enraged, renewed its assault on the cabin with terrifying ferocity. It was no longer trying to be stealthy. It threw its immense weight against the walls, making the entire structure shudder and groan. Wood splintered, nails screeched as they were torn from their holdings. The cabin was coming apart around them.

Quinn knew they couldn't stay inside. They would be crushed, or torn apart when the creature finally breached their flimsy defenses.

"Lila, we have to get out of here!" she yelled over the cacophony of the storm and the creature's assault. "The doorway! It's our only chance!"

She half-lifted, half-dragged Lila towards the broken doorway, the iron poker held ready. Lila was barely conscious, her face pale, her breathing shallow, but she clung to Quinn with a desperate strength.

As they reached the doorway, the creature, with a final, thunderous crash, tore a massive hole in the side wall of the cabin, its huge, clawed hand reaching through, flailing wildly, trying to seize them.

Quinn shoved Lila through the doorway, out into the teeth of the raging storm, then followed, stumbling, falling, into the deep, swirling snow.

They were exposed again, vulnerable, with no shelter, no defense, save for Quinn's waning strength and the rapidly fading hope that their signals had been seen.

The creature, roaring in triumph and fury, began to emerge from the ruined cabin, its massive, dark form a terrifying silhouette against the swirling whiteness.

Quinn knew this was the end. There was nowhere left to run, no strength left to fight. She pulled Lila closer, shielding her friend's body with her own, bracing for the final, inevitable assault. She closed her eyes, a prayer, a curse, a final, defiant thought forming in her mind: *We were here. We saw.*

But the killing blow did not come.

Instead, a new sound, faint at first, then growing steadily louder, cut through the howl of the storm, a sound so alien, so out of place in this primal wilderness, that Quinn thought she was hallucinating.

A rhythmic, whirring throb. A sound she had almost forgotten existed.

A helicopter.

Her eyes snapped open. Through a momentary thinning of the swirling snow, she saw it – a dark shape in the sky, its searchlight cutting a brilliant swathe through the storm, sweeping across the desolate landscape.

Hope, so fierce and unexpected it was almost painful, surged through Quinn, momentarily banishing the cold, the fear, the despair. They had been seen. They had been found.

The creature, too, had heard it. It paused in its advance, its massive head turning towards the sound, its burning eyes fixed on the approaching aircraft. It let out a deafening roar, a sound of pure, unadulterated fury and defiance, a challenge to this new, metallic intruder in its domain.

The helicopter, a Coast Guard rescue chopper, its markings just visible through the snow, descended slowly, cautiously, its searchlight illuminating the ruined cabin, the two small figures huddled in the snow, and the monstrous, terrifying shape of the creature that stood between them and salvation.

The creature did not retreat. It stood its ground, roaring its defiance, a primal force of nature confronting the encroaching world of men.

Then, with a final, earth-shattering roar, as the helicopter drew closer, its downdraft whipping the snow into a frenzy, the creature turned and, with a speed that belied its immense bulk, melted back into the deeper shadows of the forest, vanishing into the swirling whiteness as if it had never been there, leaving behind only its massive tracks in the snow and the lingering scent of primal fear.

The helicopter landed a short distance away, its rotors still spinning, its open doorway a beacon of warmth and safety. Two figures in rescue gear emerged, their faces grim as they took in the scene – the ruined cabin, the blood-stained snow, the two frostbitten, traumatized women.

Quinn felt Lila go limp beside her, her consciousness finally surrendering to the pain and exhaustion. Quinn herself could barely stand, her legs trembling, her body numb with cold and relief.

The rescuers were beside them, wrapping them in warm blankets, their voices calm, professional, reassuring. They were asking questions, but Quinn couldn't understand the words. Her mind was a maelstrom of images, of horrors, of lost friends.

She was lifted, carried towards the helicopter, towards the light, towards safety. As she was being helped inside, her gaze fell upon the GoPro camera, still clutched in her frozen hand. She had to give it to them. They had to see. They had to know.

But the effort was too much. Darkness, warm and welcoming, swarmed at the edges of her vision. She felt herself slipping away, the roar of the helicopter engines fading, the faces of her rescuers blurring.

Her last conscious thought was of the forest, of the ancient, trackless land, and the terrifying, intelligent entity that still lurked within its depths. They had been extracted. But the horror, she knew, would remain, a permanent, indelible stain on her soul. And out there, in the silent, remembering wilderness, the creature waited, its reign of terror momentarily interrupted, but far from over. The world might shrug, might dismiss, might forget. But she and Lila would know. They would always know what was still out there.

Chapter 10 – Trackless

The return to the world of the living was a jarring, painful symphony of beeping machines, hushed, urgent voices, and the sterile, antiseptic scent of a reality they had almost forgotten existed. Quinn drifted in and out of consciousness, fragments of memory – the roar of the helicopter, the blessed warmth of a blanket, Lila's limp form beside her – mingling with nightmarish flashes of burning eyes, splintering wood, and the crimson stain of blood on pristine snow.

They were in a hospital in Anchorage, the same city from which The Borealis Express had departed on its ill-fated inaugural journey what felt like a lifetime ago. Quinn's frostbite was severe, her hands and feet swathed in bandages, her face raw and peeling. Lila, in a nearby room, was battling a raging infection in her mangled leg, her life hanging by a thread for several agonizing days before the potent cocktail of antibiotics finally began to win the fight.

The questions began almost immediately, gentle at first, then more insistent, tinged with a professional skepticism that grated on Quinn's raw nerves. Doctors, nurses, somber-faced officials from the National Transportation Safety Board, representatives from Alistair Prichard's now-reeling corporation. They wanted to know what had happened. The official story was already taking shape: a catastrophic derailment due to unforeseen track instability in a remote region, exacerbated by a sudden, violent blizzard. The multiple fatalities were attributed to the crash itself, to exposure, to unfortunate encounters with territorial wildlife – bears, perhaps, or a pack of wolves, driven to desperation by the harsh conditions.

Quinn tried to tell them. She spoke of the deliberately placed logs, of the massive, intelligent creature, of the systematic, brutal cull of the passengers and crew. She described the cabin, the trapper's journal, the terrifying vocalizations, the way the entity had hunted them, toyed with them, communicated with them through horrifying, ritualistic displays.

They listened, their expressions carefully neutral, occasionally exchanging glances that Quinn couldn't quite decipher. They nodded, they took notes, they asked clarifying questions that seemed designed to highlight inconsistencies, the effects of trauma, the unreliability of memory under extreme duress. The word 'hallucination' was never explicitly used, but it hung in the air, unspoken, a suffocating blanket of disbelief.

Lila, when she was finally strong enough to speak, corroborated Quinn's account, her voice weak and trembling, her eyes haunted. But her testimony, too, was filtered through the lens of extreme trauma, her past as a social media influencer perhaps subtly undermining her credibility in their eyes. Two hysterical women, their minds broken by an unimaginable ordeal. It was a convenient, if unspoken, narrative.

The GoPro camera, which Quinn had clung to with a desperate tenacity until she lost consciousness, was taken into evidence. So was Chad's phone, its battery eventually recharged, its final, chaotic footage reviewed. The images, when Quinn was finally shown snippets by a tight-lipped investigator, were exactly what she expected: grainy, chaotic, terrifyingly suggestive but ultimately, maddeningly inconclusive.

There were fleeting glimpses of the creature from the cabin attack, a monstrous, shadowy blur in the flare's crimson light. There was the shaky, terrifying footage from Lila's camera of Marcus's abduction, a split-second movement in the trees, nothing definitive. Chad's phone had captured a few seconds of terrified screaming, the roar of the entity during the attack on Bruno, then a chaotic tumble as he fell, the lens pointing at the indifferent sky before cutting out. Screams. Shadows. A branch falling. Something moving. Nothing more.

The official report, when it was eventually released months later, was a masterpiece of bureaucratic obfuscation. It spoke of tragic loss of life, of engineering challenges in remote environments, of the unpredictable ferocity of the Alaskan wilderness. It recommended further studies, stricter protocols, enhanced safety measures. It made no mention of impossible creatures or ritualistic killings. The bodies of Hammond, Bruno, Tiffany, Chad, Kendal, Sarah, Alistair Prichard, Eleanor Ainsworth, and the dozen other passengers and crew who had perished were never found, "presumably lost to the elements or scavenged by wildlife." The forest had reclaimed its own.

The footage, however, did not remain buried in an evidence locker. How it was leaked was never determined – a disgruntled official, a curious technician, a skilled hacker

– but within weeks of Quinn and Lila's return to a semblance of physical health, it exploded onto the internet.

The Borealis Express disaster became an overnight viral sensation, a gruesome, captivating mystery for a world hungry for distraction. The grainy clips, edited and re-edited, slowed down and enhanced, set to ominous music, became the subject of endless online debate.

Conspiracy channels went into overdrive. "Bigfoot Massacre in Alaska!" screamed the headlines. "Government Cover-Up of Prehistoric Predator!" Self-proclaimed cryptozoologists and paranormal investigators dissected every frame, finding "proof" in every shadow, every ambiguous shape. They pointed to the native elder's warning, now imbued with prophetic significance. They interviewed disgruntled former employees of Prichard's company, who hinted at strange occurrences during the railway's construction, at whispers of a sacred, forbidden territory.

Mainstream media outlets covered it with a mixture of sensationalism and cautious skepticism, interviewing 'experts' who patiently debunked the creature theories. It was a bear, they said, its size exaggerated by fear and poor visibility. Or a moose, its behavior made aggressive by the rut or disease. The logs on the track? A freak natural occurrence, or perhaps the work of eco-terrorists, though no group ever claimed responsibility. The human mind, they explained, was prone to creating patterns, to seeing monsters in the dark, especially under conditions of extreme stress and trauma.

The influencer world, Lila's former domain, reacted with a predictable blend of performative horror and opportunistic content creation. There were tearful reaction videos, "RIP Borealis Express Passengers" tributes, and endless speculative vlogs. Memes proliferated: the "Alaskan Death Train," the "Bigfoot Diet Plan," Lila's terrified face from one of the clips becoming a fleeting symbol of online shock. For a week or two, it was the biggest story on the internet. Then, as quickly as it had erupted, the frenzy began to fade, replaced by the next viral outrage, the next fleeting sensation. The world shrugged, laughed, and moved on.

For Quinn and Lila, there was no moving on. They were the sole keepers of a truth too monstrous for the world to accept. The official dismissal, the online mockery, the fleeting, shallow engagement with their unimaginable trauma, was a second, more insidious kind of violation.

They retreated, by unspoken agreement, from the public eye. Lila, her leg permanently damaged, walked with a pronounced limp, a constant reminder of her ordeal. She deleted her social media accounts, abandoning the millions of followers who now either pitied her, mocked her, or clamored for more "exclusive content" from the "Bigfoot survivor." The pastel dream of her former life had been irrevocably shattered, replaced by a stark, grey reality of pain, nightmares, and the crushing weight of memory. She moved to a quiet, unassuming town in the Pacific Northwest, seeking anonymity, trying to piece together the fragments of a life that no longer made sense.

Quinn returned to the small, unassuming house she had won in the essay contest, the contest that had been her ticket to hell. The wilderness that surrounded it, once a source of solace and intellectual curiosity, now felt different, charged with a latent menace. The rustle of leaves in the wind, the snap of a twig in the woods, the distant howl of a coyote – every sound was a potential threat, a reminder of the ancient, watchful intelligence that lurked beyond the fragile boundaries of human civilization.

She, too, avoided the media, refused all interview requests. What was the point? The truth was too incredible, too horrifying. The footage, grainy and inconclusive, was all the world would ever see, and it was not enough. She poured over Octavius Becker's journal, its brittle pages a testament to a shared, recurring nightmare. She read books on folklore, on indigenous legends, on accounts of other unexplained disappearances in remote wilderness areas, searching for answers, for patterns, for anything that might help her comprehend the incomprehensible.

The nightmares were relentless. She would wake up screaming, the image of the creature's burning eyes seared into her mind, the feel of its guttural growl vibrating through her bones. The faces of her lost companions haunted her waking hours: Hammond's vacant stare, Bruno's defiant roar, Sarah's desperate, outstretched hand as she was pulled beneath the ice. The guilt of survival was a heavy cloak, a constant, suffocating presence. Why them? Why not her?

Months bled into a year. The world outside largely forgot The Borealis Express. Alistair Prichard's corporation, after settling a raft of lawsuits and paying out enormous sums in compensation, quietly shelved any plans to resurrect the ill-fated luxury train route. The Alaskan wilderness remained, vast, untamed, and indifferent, its secrets undisturbed, its ancient guardians appeased, for now.

Quinn found a fragile, tentative peace in routine, in solitude. She planted a garden, its rows of vegetables a small, defiant act of order against the encroaching chaos of her memories. She adopted a dog, a boisterous Labrador whose uncomplicated affection was a balm to her wounded soul. But the forest, the deep, dark woods that bordered her property, still called to her, a siren song of fear and fascination.

One crisp autumn afternoon, almost two years after the disaster, Quinn found herself standing at the edge of those woods. The leaves were turning, a riot of crimson and gold, beautiful and ephemeral. The air was still, holding the scent of damp earth and decaying leaves. Her dog whined softly beside her, sensing her unease.

She had not ventured far into these woods since her return. The memories were too raw, the fear too deeply ingrained. But today, something was different. A strange, unsettling calm had settled over her, a weary acceptance of the darkness that now lived within her, a permanent shadow.

She took a step, then another, pushing aside the low-hanging branches, the crunch of leaves under her boots unnaturally loud in the stillness. The dog followed, staying close to her heels, its ears pricked, its body tense.

The woods were quiet. Too quiet. No birdsong, no chatter of squirrels, just the faint sigh of the wind through the high branches. It was the same oppressive silence she remembered from the Alaskan wilderness, the silence that preceded the terror.

She walked deeper, her senses hyper-alert, every nerve ending thrumming. She was not consciously looking for anything, yet some part of her, the part that had been forged in the crucible of unimaginable horror, was searching, listening, waiting.

She came to a small clearing, dappled in the fading afternoon light. A place of quiet, almost preternatural stillness. She stopped, her gaze sweeping the surrounding trees, the dense undergrowth. Her dog let out a low, almost inaudible growl, the fur on its neck bristling slightly.

Then, it happened.

A sound, sharp and distinct, from the deeper shadows to her right. The snap of a dry twig under a heavy weight.

Quinn froze. Her heart, which had been beating with a slow, steady rhythm, leaped into her throat. Her hand instinctively went to her side, where the canister of bear spray, her constant companion, used to be. But she wasn't carrying it today. She had almost, almost, begun to feel safe.

Another sound. A soft rustle of leaves, closer this time. The distinct impression of movement, a large body shifting behind the screen of dense foliage.

The dog whined again, pressing against her legs, its body trembling.

Quinn did not move. She did not scream. She did not turn to flee. The old, familiar terror was there, a cold knot in her stomach, but it was overlaid with something else now – a profound, weary understanding. Running was futile. The wilderness remembered. The trackless places held their secrets, their ancient guardians. And sometimes, those guardians ventured beyond their appointed domains.

She stood her ground, her gaze fixed on the spot where the sound had originated. Her breath misted in the cool autumn air. She was listening, not just with her ears, but with every fiber of her being, with the part of her soul that had been irrevocably touched by the ancient, unknowable power of the wild.

The silence stretched, taut and pregnant. The dog let out another low growl, then fell silent, its body rigid with fear.

Something moved again, a subtle shift in the shadows, a darker patch against the encroaching gloom. It was there. Watching. Waiting.

Quinn did not run. She simply stood, a solitary figure in the fading light, a survivor who knew, with a certainty that transcended fear, that some tracks can never be erased, some horrors can never be truly left behind. The wilderness had marked her, and in its vast, unblinking gaze, she was, and would always be, known.

A Note from Ethan Blackwood

Thanks for diving into *Bigfoot: Trackless*. If you enjoy isolated wilderness horror with a cryptid twist, you'll definitely want to check out my novel *Shadows in the Timberline*—a fan favorite packed with tension, survival, and the haunting presence of something ancient.

See you in the woods,
Ethan

Printed in Dunstable, United Kingdom